"What do you mean?" she asked tearfully

"If you won't take the check," he said, "you'd better have something else to remember me by."

Before she realized his intention, he took her into his arms and covered her mouth with his own. Something exploded in her brain, and her lips parted under his.

How she loved him! How could anything else matter but this wondrous shared passion? But before she could speak, he thrust her away.

"Russell, I . . ."

"Spare me any more fairy tales," he said wearily. "Maybe now, instead of kissing me and pretending it was your boyfriend as you were doing at Chedoona, you'll be kissing him and wishing it was me. That will be your punishment, Shandy Farrer. Now get the hell out of my life."

Blinded by tears she groped her way to the door and did as he ordered.

VALERIE PARV had a busy and successful career as a journalist and advertising copywriter before she began writing for Harlequin in 1982. She is an enthusiastic member of several Australian writers' organizations. Her many interests include her husband, her cat and the Australian environment. Her love of the land is a distinguishing feature in many of her books for Harlequin. She has recently written a colorful study in a nonfiction book titled *The Changing Face of Australia*. Her home is in New South Wales.

Books by Valerie Parv

These books may be available at your local bookseller.

Don't miss any of our special offers. Write to us at the following address for information on our newest releases.

Harlequin Reader Service
901 Fuhrmann Blvd., P.O. Box 1397, Buffalo, NY 14240
Canadian address: P.O. Box 2800, Postal Station A,
5170 Yonge St., Willowdale, Ont. M2N 6J3

Heartbreak Plains

Valerie Parv

Harlequin Books

TORONTO • NEW YORK • LONDON
AMSTERDAM • PARIS • SYDNEY • HAMBURG
STOCKHOLM • ATHENS • TOKYO • MILAN

Original hardcover edition published in 1985
by Mills & Boon Limited

ISBN 0-373-02788-5

Harlequin Romance first edition September 1986

CHAPTER ONE

'CAN'T we go inside, just for a minute?'

At the note of appeal in her young flatmate's voice, Shandy Farrer sighed. It was Barbara's 'poor little me' voice and they both knew perfectly well that it was the one approach calculated to overcome Shandy's resistance. She glanced at her watch. 'You go ahead. I'll keep an eye out for the tram.'

Barbara pouted prettily. 'I wish you were coming with me to Noumea instead of holing up in the hills with those grotty artist types all the holidays.'

'I'm one of those grotty artist types myself,' Shandy reminded her patiently.

'Only part time. You know Miss Giles thinks of you as one of the most promising models at the Academy. "The face of the eighties, my dear",' she mimicked wickedly, then sighed. 'I wish she'd say that about me.'

At Barbara's accurate portrayal of the head of the modelling academy they both attended, Shandy was forced to laugh. 'Give yourself time, Barbie,' she advised. 'You can't expect to achieve everything just out of school. She was every bit as hard on me at the start. It's only now that I'm almost ready to graduate that she even gives me a glimmer of praise. I think she's afraid we'll get big-headed or something if she's too lavish at first. Besides, you and I look so much alike that the only real difference can be the head start I've had by being older. You'll soon catch up.'

'I suppose you're right,' Barbara agreed reluctantly, then brightened in one of her quicksilver mood changes.

'I'll just pop in for a peek. I won't even try anything on—all right?'

Again, Shandy smiled. 'Go on, then.' Keeping Barbara out of fashion boutiques was like keeping a fish away from water, and every bit as futile. The main difference between herself and Barbara was that the other girl had the money to indulge her tastes, whereas Shandy had to watch every cent. Other than that, it was true there was little physical difference between them. They had often been mistaken for sisters at the private school they'd both attended, and now at the modelling academy Shandy had chosen to fit herself for a career and at which Barbara had joined her on leaving school three years later.

Theirs was a strange friendship, Shandy mused as she stood savouring the clear spring sunshine which shone down on the pretty seaside resort of Glenelg. Their backgrounds were so different—one rich, the other decidedly working class, until Shandy's parents had won the large sum of money which changed everything. And yet, were she and Barbara so different really? They shared a common bond of loneliness—Shandy because her parents had been killed in a fire aboard a yacht they had bought without the slightest idea of how to manage it; and Barbara because her parents had been divorced when she was thirteen.

Money was partly responsible for their friendship. After their windfall, Shandy's parents had insisted on sending her to a 'good' school which she had hated until she met Barbara. The combination of Shandy's practical common sense and Barbara's boundless enjoyment of life had proved wonderfully complementary, greatly easing Shandy's way in the unfamiliar environment. When she lost her parents soon after graduating, she discovered that they had used up almost all of their winnings, leaving just enough to pay the fees at the modelling academy and keep Shandy until she could earn her living.

She had been delighted when Barbara decided to follow her to the Academy and was even more pleased when they were able to share a flat. Despite the difference in their ages, they were as close as sisters. Barbara had even risked her mother's disapproval to move into the flat. Della Stratton had been very unflattering in her opinion of Shandy, but even she mellowed once she saw what a steadying influence Shandy had on her daughter.

Nevertheless, Della kept a careful eye on both girls and was a regular visitor to the flat. Seeing the tight rein Della kept, Shandy often wondered how Barbara had ever summoned up the courage to defy her mother long enough to move away from home. It was certainly her first and last act of defiance, because after that she fell in with her forceful mother's wishes again in just about everything.

It was time to stop thinking about all that, Shandy told herself, and just enjoy the freedom of her vacation. Imagine! She had the whole month ahead of her and nothing to do but paint and paint and paint! Happily, she lifted her face and closed her eyes to enjoy the sun's golden caress, unaware of the admiring glances she drew as she did so.

If she had cared to look at her reflection in the plate-glass window at her back she would have seen what the passers-by found so appealing—a coltish long-legged blonde with golden shoulder-length hair cut in a straight fringe over a wide forehead which sloped down to where honey-gold lashes rested like silk fringes on tanned cheeks. When she did turn large, innocent blue eyes towards the window, it was not to study her own reflection. Instead, she peered through the glass, trying to locate Barbara among the racks of clothes.

'I won't be a minute,' the other girl called from inside, catching sight of Shandy looking her way. 'I just want to try on this one suit.'

She should have known that Barbara would be unable to resist trying something on. Once in the fitting room, her one suit would turn into half the garments in the boutique. Well, it would serve her right if Shandy had to leave without saying goodbye! If she didn't catch the next tram she would miss her connection with the coach which was to take her to the Flinders Ranges. Unlike Barbara, she had no hire car to collect her and take her on the first leg of her vacation.

Anxiously, she scanned Jetty Road, but there was no sign of the tram. Only a sleek black Mercedes with tinted windows cruised slowly towards her. She spared it no more than a passing glance. Glenelg was a favourite haunt of the wealthy, less now than it had once been, but luxury cars were still common enough here. She watched idly as the car slowed. No doubt the driver was looking for a particular address. Her interest was piqued when the car came to a stop at the kerb almost alongside her, and she looked to see who would get out—an actor or a pop singer, perhaps.

But the man who got out was no pop star. He looked more like a gangster in a twenties film as he looked furtively around. Shandy was tempted to laugh. Maybe he was taking part in a scene from a police drama, although she could see no cameras or film crew.

Without warning, he seized her by the arm and pulled her towards the car. 'Get in, darling.'

At first she was too stunned to be frightened. 'Hey, wait a minute!' she protested as the man reached for the suitcases at her feet.

He took no notice and pushed her through the open rear

door of the car so that she half fell onto the seat. As she tried to struggle out again he thrust her cases in after her and slammed the door. She scrabbled at it ineffectually, but the handles had been removed from the inside of the door. She opened her mouth to scream, but shock had dried her throat so much that she couldn't force out any sound.

'Don't scream or try anything,' a soft voice cautioned, and she turned to look at the man sharing the seat with her. He looked to be in his middle twenties, with a shock of boyish blonde hair and a disarming grin.

'Who are you? What do you want with me?' she croaked with an effort.

'You'll find out soon enough,' the young man said calmly. 'Co-operate and I promise you'll be quite safe.'

Safe? With these gangsters who were kidnapping her in broad daylight, snatching her from one of the most respectable suburbs in Adelaide? Hysterical laughter bubbled in her throat as they roared off at a steady speed, driven by the man who had pushed her into the car.

Something wet and warm trickled down her arm and she looked at it in dismay. Blood seeped from a graze along her forearm, sustained when she had tried to resist being forced into the car. The young man looked at the injury in concern. 'I'm sorry if you got hurt, Miss Stratton. That was unintentional, I assure you.' He took out a snowy white handkerchief and bound it around the graze. But the slight pain of the injury was swallowed up in her amazement at what he had just said. They thought she was Barbara Stratton!

At once everything fell into place. The Strattons were among the wealthiest landowners in South Australia. Barbara's father, Russell Stratton, owned a huge property west of Adelaide, somewhere along the Great Australian

Bight, she remembered now. These men had intended to kidnap Barbara, probably meaning to demand a huge ransom from her father.

What was she going to do now? Her first thought was to blurt out that they had grabbed the wrong woman; then common sense came to her aid. She had seen both their faces, so they might kill her to stop her identifying them to the police. Added to which, they had obviously known Barbara would be at the boutique at that particular time, so they might go back and try again. She decided it was safer for both girls if she kept her mouth shut for the time being. This way she might be able to learn more about her abductors. At the very least she could buy Barbara enough time to get away before the men discovered their mistake. What would happen to her then, she shuddered to think. When Barbara's father received the ransom demand he would call the resort in Noumea and would soon know that his daughter was safe. He would probably guess that the girl being held was Barbara's flatmate, but there was no reason why he should care what happened to her after that.

A sigh that was half sob shook her, and she jumped as the young man reached across to her. But it was only to pat her hand reassuringly. 'I told you we won't hurt you, Miss Stratton. Don't be scared.'

The concern in his voice surprised her. She didn't know how she expected kidnappers to act, but it certainly wasn't with such sympathy. Perhaps the older man was the ringleader and the younger one was only following orders, perhaps even against his will. If so, he might take her side if she tried to escape. She realised she was pinning a lot on a slight gesture, but it was the only hope she had.

'What's your name?' she asked the young man quietly.

'Robin Crossley,' he said at once, and she swallowed hard. She hadn't expected him to give his full name. She shot a nervous glance at the driver, but he didn't react when his accomplice spoke, so the name was probably false. Her hopes plummeted. But what had she expected—their real names and addresses?

'Which do you prefer?' Robin was asking.

'I'm sorry?'

'A lot of girls called Barbara prefer a nickname, like Barbie or Barb.'

'Oh, I see. Well, actually, my friends call me Shandy.' At least it wasn't a lie, and lots of people had unusual nicknames. Hers had been given to her by her father who thought Charlotte—her real name—was too big a mouthful for the undersized infant she had been when her mother chose it. 'Besides,' her father told her later, 'you were always like a glass of shandy—a mix of bubbling innocence and intoxicating spirit.'

'Shandy,' Robin repeated thoughtfully. 'Unusual, but it suits you. Glad to meet you, Shandy Stratton.'

'I . . . I wish I could say the same,' she ventured. 'Where are you taking me?'

He smiled but without malice. 'Ah, that would be telling. It's kind of a surprise, in a way.'

You're telling me! she thought hysterically. This was the kind of surprise she wished she could wake up from, to find that it had all been a ghastly nightmare.

The car slowed a little and she looked out through the tinted window. They were driving towards an intersection and there was some kind of traffic hold-up ahead. They passed a policeman who was trying to sort out the traffic snarl, and her heart leapt. But there was no way she could attract his attention. Beyond the hold-up, which turned out to be a minor collison between two cars, they picked up speed again. From the surroundings, she realised they were heading for the airport.

Her hopes began to rise again as the driver swung the car into the busy airport complex and turned into one of the large car parks. Here, surely, there would be someone she could appeal to for help. If, as she guessed, they planned to take her somewhere by plane, she would have the few minutes between car and tarmac to try to attract attention.

But when they got out of the car, the driver started off towards the terminal building alone. When she started to follow, Robin Crossley took a gentle but firm grip on her arm. 'We'll wait here.'

Disappointed, she sagged against the car. 'Why are you doing this?' she asked miserably.

'Boss's orders,' he said cryptically. 'Don't worry, it'll all make sense soon.'

Instead of being reassured by his words, she found her apprehension deepening. Who was 'the Boss?' And what other orders had he given concerning her? 'Look . . . Robin,' she appealed with an edge of desperation in her voice, 'you seem much too nice to be a kidnapper. I . . . I'm sure you didn't have any choice, but . . . but we're alone now. Can't you let me go?'

He grinned. 'Thanks for the compliment. But no, we'll wait here till Les gets back.'

She bit her lip to stop the tears from coming. If only someone would come back to one of the sea of cars surrounding them! Then miraculously a young couple started towards them. At once she spun away from the car. 'Help, please!' she called, although she wasn't sure whether they were within hearing range yet. Before she could run towards them, Robin took hold of her arm and yanked her back against him.

Sensing her opportunity slipping away, she threw back her head and forced air into her lungs which were crushed by Robin's embrace. 'Help! I'm being kidn . . .'

Her words were muffled by the sudden contact of his lips with hers as he swept her into what looked, to anyone watching, like a lover's farewell. She could have wept with frustration as she heard the couple's footsteps pass by only yards away. There was the jangle of keys, the slam of car doors, then the cough of an engine coming to reluctant life.

Robin waited until the car had driven off before he released her. 'You're despicable,' she spat at him.

He shook his head. 'Just expedient.' He licked his lips thoughtfully. 'Care to try that again?'

'I could kill you,' she seethed, not sure whether he was referring to her attempted escape or the stolen kiss.

'Maybe you shouldn't give your kidnapper ideas,' he said gravely.

She felt the colour drain from her face. What was she thinking of, provoking him like this when there was every chance he could carry out such a threat? She turned away from him, thankful for the car's support because her legs felt ready to give out. If she was to get out of this alive, she had better watch what she said to him—or to his mysterious boss, whoever he was. 'I . . . I'm sorry,' she said with an effort.

'I'm not,' he said with maddening good cheer, 'I rather enjoyed shutting you up.'

Just then, the man called Les came back with a folder of papers in his hand. He nodded to Robin. 'We're all set.'

Robin took her arm in a grip which brooked no argument, and Les lifted her meagre luggage out of the car, locked it, then stood on the other side of her. 'Let's go.'

Her plan to attract attention in the busy terminal was

thwarted when they avoided the main building altogether and walked to a much smaller hangar alongside the main terminal. Here, a small executive jet was waiting. Her heart sank as Robin escorted her towards it and helped her aboard.

Once the heavy cabin door was closed, neither Robin nor Les stopped her moving about the small, luxuriously appointed cabin. Where could she go anyway? In despair, she slumped into one of the armchair-like seats and hardly looked up when Robin expertly snapped a safety belt across her lap. 'Cheer up, won't be long now,' he assured her.

He was right. Les had apparently taken care of any departure formalities, and in minutes she felt the small plane taxi to a runway and start the headlong rush which preceded take-off. The floor tilted and she was pressed against the deeply upholstered seat, then they were airborne, her last chance of escape gone.

The memory of Robin's unwelcome kiss stung her lips like a brand, and she scrubbed the back of one hand across her mouth to try to erase the feel of it. The few times she had been kissed in her life, had amounted to no more than a casual peck. Only once had a boyfriend tried to take matters further and she had struggled free in disgust. It wasn't that she was afraid of sexual contact—more that she put such a high value on it that she would have felt she was cheating herself if she treated it lightly. She guessed she was 'saving herself' for the right man, to use the old-fashioned expression.

Robin's kiss had violated her sense of what was right, and she knew she would not forgive him for it. But what if it did not stop there? What if . . . her mind refused to accept the possibility that kidnappers could also be rapists. They couldn't . . . they wouldn't . . .

To force her mind on to something else, she stared fixedly out of the plane window. Perhaps she could memorise some of the countryside in case she had to help the police locate their hideout if . . . when . . . she was rescued.

There wasn't a lot to be seen at first. Fluffy strands of white and pink-tinged cloud obscured most of the landscape below. But now and then she caught a glimpse of deeply indented coastline and white-flecked ocean. From the position of the sun, they were flying west along the coastline. The plane began to lose height steadily until she could make out more of the landforms below. Rushing up to meet them was a great jagged triangle jutting out into the Southern Ocean—the Eyre Peninsula! She was sure she recognised it, and the discovery cheered her. The tip of the land triangle was barbed to form Boston Bay and Coffin Bay with a long length of coastline along Spencer Gulf and the unmistakable sweep of the Great Australian Bight. Perhaps their hideout was somewhere along the vast, empty Nullarbor Plains which bordered the Bight.

As the land rushed up to meet them she glimpsed an expanse of flat, cultivated country which gave way to red-sand plains stretching from horizon to horizon, its low cover of spinifex and mallee scrub and lack of rivers making it look bleak and desolate. She shivered. Who would ever find her here?

She had time to glimpse a cluster of low-lying buildings beyond a line of hills; then they came in to land and the tyres threw up showers of dust from a bush airstrip. The jet taxied to a halt near a Range Rover, the only sign of human activity for miles.

Robin unfastened his seatbelt, then leaned across to undo hers. He stood up and stretched luxuriously. 'Okay, young Shandy, time to meet the Boss.'

Her fear came rushing back and she stumbled in climbing out of the aircraft, so that Robin had to help her. She glanced over her shoulder, but it seemed that Les was staying aboard.

The Range Rover was also deserted when they reached it, but as Robin tried to assist her into the front seat, she dug her heels in. 'No, not until you tell me where we're going and who this . . . your Boss is.'

He cocked an eyebrow. 'You still don't know where you are? Oh well, I guess it has been a few years.'

A few years? Was she supposed to recognise this desolate countryside? Then she remembered she was pretending to be Barbara, who might well have known the place. 'I . . . er . . . yes, quite a few years,' she improvised. Since she had very little choice, she climbed into the vehicle and settled herself in the front seat, while Robin moved around to the driver's side.

In tense silence, they followed a gravel road towards the low line of hills she had seen from the plane and beyond which she had spotted a homestead of some sort. She braced herself for her first meeting with Robin's Boss.

As they crested the line of hills, she gave an involuntary gasp of pleasure. Spread out before them was a green oasis amid the saltbush and mallee. Around the outside of the settlement were structures which must be farm buildings—a machinery shed of some sort, what looked like a woolshed, cattleyards and stables. Dominating the scene was a handsome stone house which seemed curiously at one with the landscape around it. Although the outbuildings were modern, the house looked as if it had stood where it was for a century or more, exuding an atmosphere of restfulness, as if it was conscious of its period heritage. There was a suggestion of Cornish farmhouse about it, but the blue-tinged stone came from somewhere local, because she could see the stone reflected in the ground itself. The artist in her responded to the beauty and tranquillity of the homestead, and a smile of appreciation crept over her face.

'Ah, I see you do know where you are,' Robin stated, misinterpreting her reaction. 'I'll let you settle in before I try and apologise for bringing you here like this. After you've spoken to the Boss and understand his reasons, maybe you'll even forgive me for the airport.'

She kept her expression carefully impassive, although her mind was whirling. Obviously, she was expected to know where she was, but Robin's words had only made her more confused than ever. Apparently, she was also expected to know who the Boss was. If that was the case, why didn't he just issue a polite invitation to Barbara, instead of snatching her . . . or rather, Shandy . . . like this? 'We'll see,' she said firmly, in response to his statement.

He shrugged. 'As you like. But I'll be very disappointed if the Boss's daughter turns out to be a stuck-up little madam like her mother.'

The Boss's daughter! Oh lord, this must be Chedoona Downs, Barbie's family home which Shandy had heard her flatmate talk about. If so, the Boss must be Russell Stratton, Barbara's father—which still didn't explain why he would need to kidnap his own daughter.

She tried frantically to recall what Barbara had said about her father, and realised now that she hadn't talked about him much at all. Della had been more outspoken, but she seldom had a kind word for her ex-husband. From her, Shandy had gained the impression that Russell Stratton was an implacable tyrant, which was why Della had been unable to go on living with him. His action in having

'Barbara' snatched from the street and brought to him seemed to confirm this image of him, Shandy thought with a shiver of apprehension.

Now that she knew she wasn't in the hands of criminals, she was no longer frightened, but she was unsure of her reception in the Stratton household. It seemed unlikely that she would get a warm welcome, even though none of this was her fault.

It *was* Robin's fault, she thought with a sudden surge of anger. She turned blazing eyes on him. 'Why didn't you tell me you were bringing me here?' she demanded.

He shrugged, keeping his eyes on the rutted track. 'Boss's orders, like I said.'

'If he told you to jump off the Bight, I suppose you'd do that, too?'

'Luckily for me, he doesn't give orders without good reason,' he said, avoiding a direct answer.

What would be his good reason on this occasion, she wondered moodily. Because it had better be good. She wasn't one of the Boss's boot-licking employees and she intended to give him a very large slice of her mind before demanding to be taken back to Adelaide.

In this aggressive mood, she got out of the car and stalked to the front door, which was shaded by long, low eaves and a wide verandah. At the sound of the car pulling up, the flyscreen had been flung open and a woman emerged wiping floury hands on a patchwork apron. She was an attractive woman, about forty Shandy judged, although she had looked after her figure and skin which were those of a younger woman. Her sleek dark hair was only slightly greying at the temples. This, plus the few strands of hair escaping from the chignon at her nape, made her look almost girlish. Shandy warmed to her instinctively.

'Rob, your timing is perfect,' the woman smiled. 'I was just putting the kettle on.'

Robin bent slightly to give the woman a peck on the cheek. 'Hello, Mum. I'm not staying for tea, thanks. I have to check in with the Boss.'

'He's in the North Paddock,' the woman informed him.

Meanwhile, Shandy stood to one side resisting the urge to tap her foot with impatience. At last Robin remembered she was there. 'Mum, this is Barbara Stratton. Shandy, meet my mother, Helen Crossley, the Boss's housekeeper.'

Helen Crossley enveloped Shandy's hand in both of hers, and the warmth communicated itself to Shandy at once. Here, she could sense she had an ally. 'Welcome home, Miss Stratton. Of course, you don't know me—I've only been here two years, long after you and your mother . . . went away.'

Which was a tactful way of alluding to the divorce, Shandy thought. She was glad the housekeeper was a newcomer so that she didn't have to explain who she was just yet. She would prefer to do that with Russell himself. After that, she probably wouldn't be staying long enough for the staff to require explanations.

'I'll leave you in Mum's tender care,' Robin said. He lifted her luggage out of the Range Rover and stacked it on the verandah, then drove off in a flurry of dust.

Shandy reached for one of the cases but was forestalled by the housekeeper. 'None of that,' she admonished with mock sternness. 'Or I'll have my union on you.' Carrying both cases as if they weighed nothing, she led the way inside.

After the warmth outdoors, the interior of the house was blissfully cool and Shandy let out a deep sigh. Mrs

Crossley looked at her in concern. 'Tired, dear?'

'Yes, it's been a . . . a long day.'

'Then I'll take you right up to your room so you can rest and freshen up before dinner. Would you like a cup of tea brought up?'

'Yes, please,' she agreed, tasting it already. 'What time will Mr . . . er . . . the Boss be back?'

'In time for dinner, he told me. Anxious to see him again?' the housekeeper asked her.

If you only knew! Shandy thought. 'Something like that,' she dissembled.

She followed the housekeeper up a broad timber staircase which glowed from years of polishing, into the most enchanting bedroom she had ever seen. For a fleeting moment, she wished she *was* Barbara Stratton, with the right to stay in the restful room, instead of in a rough timber cabin with the other artists in the Flinders Ranges.

The room was wallpapered in a small green-and-pink rose print set off by vertical beams of oiled timber supporting shelves of temptingly bound books. The pink was repeated in a Victorian china water jug set atop an old timber dresser. Everything was perfect, down to the filmy curtains and huge brass bedstead with its hand-made lace coverlet. 'What a lovely room,' she breathed, forgetting that she was supposed to have grown up here.

To her relief, the housekeeper smiled. 'I'm glad you like the new colours. Mr Stratton chose them himself for in here.' Before Shandy could think of a suitable reply, Mrs Crossley set her cases down beside the bed. 'I'll leave you to settle in, dear. The tea won't be long and dinner is at seven.'

She returned with the tea almost at once, and when she had gone, Shandy sipped it, frowning. It looked as if she might have to spend the night here after all. By the time she and Russell Stratton had exchanged explanations, it would be too late for her to return to Adelaide. She wasn't even sure if the pilot known as Les was coming back with the plane tonight. She had heard him take off again as soon as she and Robin drove away in the Range Rover.

Suddenly weary, she sank down onto the bed. What a day it had been! The pillows banked up behind her looked very tempting, but she sat up again determinedly. She had better not make herself too much at home here, in case Russell Stratton got the idea that she had encouraged the deception.

A tour of the room revealed a modern bathroom opening off one side, and a huge built-in wardrobe filled with the most gorgeous clothes Shandy had ever seen. During her model's training, she had seen enough designer clothes to recognise a top label when she saw one, and she suppressed a twinge of envy at the thought of owning such lovely things.

Which reminded her—she had better find something suitable to wear to meet Russell Stratton. The figure-hugging jeans and checked cotton shirt might be all right for the artists' colony, but she had a feeling that Russell Stratton would disapprove of such informality, and they had enough problems to resolve without antagonising him if she could avoid it.

After the glimpse of the garments in the closet, her own limited wardrobe seemed less appealing than ever. She looked speculatively at the wardrobe. Dare she? It *was* Russell Stratton's fault that she was in this fix with nothing suitable to wear.

That decided it. She returned to the rack of dresses—all noticeably new—and selected a trim, bib-fronted dress in a stylish lemon stripe iced with white. Luckily she and

Barbara were the same size, so it fitted like a dream and the silky fabric felt cool against her skin.

Sliding out of the dress again, she hurried through a shower and then spent ten minutes brushing her golden hair until it gleamed. Then, wearing the model dress once more, and with her own leather sandals on bare feet— Stratton's providence didn't stretch to stockings, or at least none that she could find—she felt ready to face the Boss himself.

She located the dining room easily enough. It was a grand room with oregon beamed ceiling and cool slate floor, and a table which looked as if it could seat a dozen people. Tonight, it was set for only two. There was no sign of her host as yet, so she meandered around the big room, glorying in its olde-worlde ambience.

Her artist's eye was drawn to a portrait hanging on the wall above a massive stone fireplace. Although the subject couldn't have been more than twelve, she recognised Barbara at once and moved closer to admire the skilled brushwork. The sound of footsteps behind her made her stiffen with apprehension.

'Barbara! You're here at last!'

Unable to delay the moment any longer, she turned reluctantly and was confronted with a towering man whose air of absolute mastery identified him at once as Russell Stratton.

She studied him quickly, seeking some reassuring likeness to Barbara but finding none. His brooding good looks with glossy black hair and thick eyebrows reminded her of an approaching thunderstorm. Broad shoulders tapered to a narrow waist and athletic hips, creating an impression of great strength and power, carefully leashed, while the luminous blue-black eyes he directed at Shandy suggested both rogue and lover. But the twisted smile above a craggy cleft chin held no warmth at all. Instead, his eyes flashed fire as he folded his arms across his chest and glared at her furiously.

'Who the hell are you?'

CHAPTER TWO

ALTHOUGH every instinct urged her to turn and run from the man's dominating presence, she stepped forward and held out her hand. 'I'm Charlotte Farrer, your daughter's flatmate, Mr Stratton.'

He ignored the outstretched hand and continued to scrutinise her coldly. 'At least you've got the guts to be honest with me, young lady—although you let my staff believe you were my daughter.'

The unfairness of this accusation shattered her poise, and she took a step backwards. 'I didn't tell them I was Barbara—they just assumed . . .'

'. . . assumed for eight hundred kilometres!' he said sarcastically. 'Surely some time along the way the truth could have slipped out?'

It was too much! The hours of travelling, when her nerves were stretched to breaking point, believing she was in the hands of criminals, had all taken their toll. The last shreds of her self-control snapped. 'Now look here, Mr Stratton,' she exploded, 'this morning, I was standing in Jetty Road, waiting for a tram and minding my own business, when your . . . your thugs . . . dragged me off the street and into a car, hurting me into the bargain. When I realised they were after Barbara, I thought the best thing I could do to protect both of us was to keep quiet. For all I knew they could have killed me and gone back for her. And this is the thanks I get!'

To her horror, she dissolved into tears as the day's pent-up emotions were finally given full rein. She took

24

deep gulps of air to try to control the sobs racking her slight frame, but the tears continued to flow as if they would never stop.

To her surprise, Russell Stratton strode across the room and placed an arm around her heaving shoulders, then led her to a couch and pushed her firmly onto it.

When she tried to get up again, he pushed her back down. 'I'm s-sorry,' she gasped. 'I c-can't seem to s-stop crying.'

'I'm the one who should be sorry,' he assured her grimly, his anger now directed at himself. 'I should've realised how it would appear to you. Of course, Barbara would have recognised where she was as soon as the plane flew over Ceduna, so the experience wouldn't have been as distressing for her as it must have been for you.' A well-stocked bar occupied one corner of the room. He went to it and poured two drinks, then handed one of them to her. 'Drink this. It will help to steady your nerves.'

She looked at it distrustfully. 'What is it?'

'Good old-fashioned whisky.'

She downed it in one swallow like medicine, and grimaced. 'Ugh! How can people drink that stuff for pleasure?'

He smiled at her reaction, and the transformation was startling. The angles and planes of his face softened at once, and Shandy realised with a start that he was a very good-looking man. He must have been very young when he married Della, because he only looked to be in his late thirties now.

'At least you've stopped looking at me as though I'm some sort of monster,' he said.

She blushed as she became aware that she was staring at him. 'No, I . . . I didn't think that,' she said in confusion. 'It must be the whisky.'

'Thanks,' he murmured drily.

She blushed even more furiously. 'Oh, sorry, I . . . I didn't mean it was *only* the whisky . . .'

He waved a hand dismissively. 'Never mind. It seems I owe you an apology for today—and an explanation.'

'Well, I do want to know why you didn't just *invite* Barbara to come here, instead of abducting me . . . her.'

He sighed deeply. 'It's a long story. Would you have dinner with me while I tell you?'

She nodded agreement, uncomfortably reminded that she hadn't eaten since breakfast, which now seemed like an eternity ago. Robin Crossley had offered her some sandwiches on the plane, but she had been too distraught to even think of eating. Now she was ravenously hungry. She stood up quickly and swayed. On an empty stomach, the unaccustomed whisky had gone straight to her head, so she felt very light-headed. 'I think I'd better eat something,' she said to Russell Stratton.

He took her arm and helped her to the table. 'I think you better had, Miss Farrer—or may I call you Charlotte?'

'My friends call me Shandy,' she offered.

'Then I hope you'll include me among them after we get this misunderstanding sorted out?' Without quite knowing why, she had a feeling that she would, and nodded shyly. 'Good. Shandy, it is then—and I'm Russell, or Russ as you prefer.' He extended his hand and this time they shook hands solemnly. She gained an impression of great strength in his carefully restrained grip.

Although she was anxious to hear his explanation for the extraordinary events of the day, he waved aside her questions while Helen Crossley served their meal.

They began with a garden salad garnished with scallops and ginger which Shandy found piquant and unusual.

When she said so, Russell smiled. 'Helen Crossley is an outstanding cook. Farm fare is usually much more basic, so I'm lucky to have her.'

The main course was a succulent rack of lamb garnished with fresh tarragon and mint. There must be a thriving herb garden on the property, Shandy decided.

Between courses, Russell Stratton plied her with questions about the Academy and her career. 'What do your parents think of your modelling?' he asked.

She looked quickly down at her plate. 'They were killed just after I left school.'

He covered her hand in a spontaneous gesture of sympathy. 'I'm so sorry. Was it a car?'

She shook her head and, to her surprise, found herself pouring out the tragic story of the sudden windfall which had changed her family's life. 'They'd never had much money before, so it went to their heads,' she said bitterly. 'They bought everything they'd ever wanted, showered me with gifts—more than I could ever use. We were so happy before, when they were poor.'

'You sound as if you blame the money for their deaths.'

Her eyes clouded at the memory. 'Oh, I do! If it hadn't been for that, they'd never have bought that hateful boat. Imagine—Mum and Dad on a yacht! Mum wouldn't even trust herself on a ferry before.'

'What happened?' he prompted gently.

'Some cooking oil caught fire in the galley. The boat burned to the waterline,' she said flatly. 'They didn't have a chance.'

'Poor Shandy. No other relatives?'

'No. Mum and Dad were both only children. It's all right, though. I've had time to adjust. Of course, I still miss them terribly but . . . you have to pick up the pieces and go on, don't you? They left just enough for me to live on for a while, and pay the fees at the Academy, so I'll have a career to fall back on.'

He raised an eyebrow. 'To fall back on? Then modelling isn't your first choice of career?'

'No, I . . . I really want to be an artist.'

He nodded in understanding. 'You have talent?'

She had asked herself this question often enough to be objective about it. 'Yes, I think so. But it's a precarious way to make a living. At least modelling pays well and doesn't tie you down to a nine-to-five existence.' She shuddered at the idea.

'Were you going to spend your vacation painting?'

'The whole month!' Unaware of how her eyes began to sparkle as she talked about her first love, she told him about the artists' colony where she had planned to spend her vacation. 'It's near Melrose, an enchanting place at the foot of the Flinders Ranges—you know, Hans Heysen country.'

'I know it,' Russell acknowledged. 'I have a Heysen here as a matter of fact. I must show it to you after dinner.'

'I'd like that. I admire him so much. My style has been compared to his—something about the way I handle light and shade. And I love landscapes, of course. Not that I'd compare myself to Heysen,' she said quickly, 'but if I can ever be half as accomplished . . .'

'I understand. This colony you were bound for—do you have to book, like a motel?'

She laughed at the very idea. 'Goodness, no! Colony sounds impressive, but it's just a collection of timber cabins and a communal dining room on the banks of Campbell's Creek. It's run by an art teacher I used to study with, Jordan Cole. That's how I found the place. Anybody who calls themselves an artist can just wander in anytime. If there's a bunk free, it's yours.'

'It doesn't sound like the sort of place your parents would have approved of,' he said seriously.

'Oh, but it's very moral—Jordan sees to that. He's very strict. You're only allowed to stay there if you mean to work. There's no . . . no hanky-panky, or anything.'

'I see. So no-one there was expecting you?' Russell asked carefully.

Before she could reply to this, Helen Crossley came bustling in with glasses of strawberry sorbet. Shandy waved hers away. 'It looks wonderful, but I just couldn't.'

'That's all right. The country air will soon sharpen your appetite,' Helen Crossley said kindly. 'You could use a little feeding up.'

Shandy shot a glance of surprise at Russell. Apparently, he hadn't told his housekeeper about the misunderstanding yet, so she still believed Shandy was staying with them for a while. Well, it wasn't up to her to interfere between him and his staff, so she said nothing. Mrs Crossley would find out tomorrow anyway.

When the housekeeper had gone, she turned to her host. 'We've done nothing but talk about me. I think it's your turn.'

He spread his hands wide and smiled, disarming her. 'But I'm not half so interesting—or attractive.' Then he grew serious and reached across to fill her glass with more champagne, before going on. 'You know that Della and I were divorced when Barbara was twelve?'

'Yes, Barbie told me—and Della . . . has spoken of you.'

A frown creased his forehead. 'I can imagine in what way. We were both too young when we married—I was nineteen and she was barely eighteen.'

So she had been right! 'You don't have to tell me about it,' she assured him.

'Yes, I do. It will help you to understand why I couldn't

just ask Barbara to come here. You see, when Della left me . . .'

Shandy started in surprise. 'Left you, but . . .'

'I know. That was not the way you heard it, I'm sure. But that's the way it happened. She was bored with the country life and wanted to return to the city. Barbara was very young and impressionable when Della took her away, so it wasn't hard to poison her against me. Della convinced her that I had sent them away because I didn't want them any more.'

'But I'm sure she doesn't think that!' Shandy said at once, although there was no conviction in her tone. It explained why Barbara was so reluctant to talk about her father or anything that happened before she came to Adelaide with Della.

He watched her face for a moment. 'Yes, she does,' he said sadly, 'and I see you know it too. But I didn't want her to spend her life hating me, so I decided it was time she knew my side of the story.'

'So you were going to bring her here forcibly, and make her listen.'

'Yes. It was the only way I could get her alone, away from her mother's influence. I was sure I could make her understand, given a little time.'

Shandy's eyes filled with tears of sympathy for him. 'What a mess! Now your only chance to spend some time with her is gone because I was in the wrong place at the wrong time.'

He smiled wryly. 'It was hardly your fault, Shandy. The physical resemblance is quite remarkable, and you believed you were doing the right thing by not revealing who you really were.'

'At first, when your men bundled me into the car, I was too frightened to say anything. Then when they called me

Miss Stratton, I thought they meant to kidnap her and hold her for ransom. All I could think was, if they found out they'd grabbed the wrong woman, they might go back for Barbara, and she's not . . . not as strong as I am.'

'What you mean is she's fragile and spoilt,' he corrected. Then he raised his champagne glass in a toast. 'You acted very bravely today, Shandy. I salute you. But remind me to tell Robin not to be so melodramatic about things in future. I think he got a bit carried away with the cloak-and-dagger stuff today.'

'You can say that again,' Shandy said ruefully, rubbing the graze on her arm. 'He calls you The Boss—does he work for you?'

'That's right. The other man you . . . er . . . met, was Les Archer, my pilot and driver when I'm in Adelaide. Robin is the manager of Chedoona Downs, but only under my guidance, until he gains more practical experience. His father died two years ago, just before Robin graduated from Agricultural College. When the estate was settled Rob and his mother found that their property was mortgaged to the hilt and had to be sold to settle the debts. Robin's determined to buy it back some day. I offered to finance the purchase for him, but the most he would accept was work for himself and his mother and a home for them both here.'

'How awful for them,' Shandy said. Her heart went out to Robin whom she liked instinctively, despite the unfortunate manner of their meeting. She was also impressed by Russell Stratton's obvious concern for his neighbours. It was getting harder and harder to associate this strong, gentle man with the tyrant Della made him out to be.

Her eyes strayed to his hands, resting lightly on either side of his champagne glass. They were strong, capable hands, the sinews standing out clearly and the nails neatly trimmed ovals rounding off long fingers—not what she would have envisaged for a farmer, she thought idly. She would enjoy painting his hands just as they were now. Better yet, she would like to feel them caressing her with firm gentleness. What would it be like to have his hands on her, to be held in the strong circle of his arms? She had never met a man who exuded such strength and masculinity. Astonished at herself, she shook her head to dispel such thoughts. It must be the whisky before dinner and the champagne during it, which was giving her such outrageous fantasies. She would have to watch herself, she thought dreamily. Russell was much too good-looking and charming. Luckily, she would only be around him until tomorrow. Until then, she would have to remind herself he was Barbara's father, and only putting up with Shandy to make amends for this morning.

'I'm sorry . . . what did you say?'

He smiled at her inattention. 'I said I can understand Robin's mistake. You do look very like Barbara in a superficial way. But you are much more compassionate and caring than she is.'

'Oh, but Barbara's really very sweet when you get to know her.' She saw his expression harden. 'I'm sorry, I forgot—you haven't had the chance, have you?'

'I'm afraid not. But I've kept an eye on her from a distance, and she writes to me out of duty, I suppose. She's her mother's daughter—more's the pity. Perhaps I should have fought harder to keep her, but I believed Della. She convinced me that the property was too isolated for a young girl just entering her teens, so I let Della take her away. I believed Della too readily, in too many things.'

His expression grew distant, and the fingers gripping his glass tightened, the knuckles whitening, until the fragile crystal snapped, spilling the remaining few drops of liquid. Shandy was startled by the intensity of his feelings.

He looked at the shattered glass and spilled wine as if seeing it for the first time. When Shandy reached across to mop up the wine with her napkin he pushed her hand away.

'Leave it. I'll have Helen take care of it. I shouldn't let the past affect me so strongly.'

'I guess it affects all of us to some degree,' Shandy ventured softly, 'luckily not always for bad. You can have good memories too—they're the ones to cherish.'

His eyes widened as he regarded her with new respect. 'You're very wise for one . . .'

So young? she anticipated, feeling a twinge of sadness. Somehow, she didn't want to be reminded of the difference in their ages right now.

'. . . for one so lovely,' he finished, warming her, although she was sure that wasn't what he had intended to say. Perhaps he didn't want to shatter their pleasant sense of camaraderie either.

'By the way,' he said, interrupting her thoughts, 'that dress looks stunning on you.'

She coloured guiltily. 'I hope you didn't mind me helping myself from Barbara's wardrobe. The clothes I have with me were chosen for a painting trip.'

'Not at all. I bought them all for Barbara, so feel free to wear any of them you like—you can keep any that particularly take your fancy.'

'Oh, I couldn't think of it!' she demurred. 'I just needed something suitable for tonight, that's all.'

He stood up. 'How would you like me to show you the house? We can start with the gallery—and the Heysen.'

She followed him out of the dining room and along a hallway. Opening off it, she glimpsed an office, a long sleepout adjoining it, and a large airy room which looked as if it had been designed as a children's playroom. She felt a stab of sorrow for Russell Stratton. Such a room should be filled with running, squealing children. Barbara must, indeed, have been a lonely child here. Russell followed the direction of her gaze. 'That was the nursery,' he explained shortly. 'This house was meant for a very large family.'

'Has your family lived here for long?' she asked, intrigued by the warm, secure character of the house and its unmistakable air of permanence.

'There have been Strattons here since the 1880s,' he told her with a ring of pride in his voice, 'or rather Strathopoulos's. My multi-great-grandfather was one of the first Greek settlers in Australia.'

This accounted for his dark complexion and aquiline features, she thought. They emerged into a long, narrow room which appeared to have been combined out of two smaller ones. Along one wall, bay windows looked out onto a darkened landscape while the other walls were hung with an impressive collection of paintings. The Heysen, she spotted at once. It had pride of place down one end of the gallery, and she moved closer to inspect it. The glowing world of reds and ochres it depicted could only be the Flinders Ranges as seen through the eye and brush of the famous landscape artist.

'It's lovely,' she breathed, appreciating the skilled composition which showed a rocky creek-bed studded with majestic river gums, against a backdrop of craggy outcrops and towering peaks becoming hazy in the distance. 'To be able to do so much with watercolours!' she said with a touch of envy.

Russell Stratton stretched out in a leather armchair and watched as she made her round of the gallery. 'Take your time,' he urged.

She soon forgot that he was watching her as she became absorbed in the collection. Once, her eye was caught by the signature, Theo Stratton, scrawled at the bottom of a seascape. To her critical eye, the technique was primitive, but full of promise. 'A relative?' she asked, turning to Russell.

'My grandfather,' he confirmed. 'He was a seaman at heart, and the few times he exercised his talent for art, it was to paint the sea in all her moods. He left the land for it in the end and was one of the founders of our fishing port of Thevenard.'

'So your family aren't all farmers?' she queried.

'Far from it. Mine is the only branch that has taken to the land.'

'The others?'

'Pirates,' he said, obviously relishing her startled reaction.

'You're kidding,' she said.

'No, I'm quite serious. That was how we got to Australia. My great-great-great-great grandfather, Adonis Strathopoulos, was among the crew of a Greek schooner which held up a British brig and stole her cargo. There was no violence, but it was still an Act of Piracy. They were caught, taken to Malta for trial, and sentenced to transportation to Australia. Later, he earned his freedom, married and became an Australian, changing the family name to Stratton.'

'What a thrilling history,' she enthused, thinking how appropriate it was that Russell should be descended from pirates. It was easy to imagine him dressed in tight knee-breeches and flowing Regency shirt, standing astride the deck of a Greek schooner. Loyal to his friends, merciless to his enemies, brigand . . . lover, a small voice whispered.

'Come back to me, Shandy!' he commanded, snapping his fingers. He laughed at her faraway expression. 'What were you thinking of just now?'

'Oh . . . er . . . nothing,' she stammered.

He reached across to push a strand of hair back from her forehead. 'Confess! You were picturing me in the role of my buccaneer ancestor.'

'I was not!' she said hotly, but her heightened colour gave the lie to her denial. 'All right, I was. You're the first pirate I've ever met.'

'I'm not sure whether to be flattered or insulted,' he mused. 'Remember, we Strattons stopped being pirates rather abruptly, when we became guests of the British Government in Australia. I might take it up again, though. Looting, pillage and rape would make a change from running Chedoona Downs. In a way, I've already started—after all, I did carry off my first fair maiden today, didn't I?'

She avoided his eyes, but part of her thrilled to the caressing way he called her 'fair maiden'. It made her feel very much like a woman. She decided it was time for a change of subject. 'May I see the rest of the house now?'

'Tomorrow,' he assured her. 'It's late, and I'm sure you must be exhausted after your trying day.'

'Oh, but I won't have time tomorrow,' she said, disappointed. 'I'll have to fly back to Adelaide first thing and try to arrange a seat on another coach to the Ranges.'

His teasing expression was replaced by a seriousness which alarmed her. 'I'm afraid you won't be going back to Adelaide just yet,' he said quietly.

She stared at him in disbelief. 'What do you mean—I won't be going back?'

'It's very simple,' he explained. 'If I let you go back

now, there's nothing to stop you going to the police and having me charged with kidnapping.'

She felt as if the floor was tilting under her, and steadied herself against a wall. 'I wouldn't do that,' she said, aghast at the very idea. 'I admit, I was frightened at first, but now that I understand why you resorted to such a thing . . .'

'It doesn't change anything. Whether I had good reason or not, I arranged to have you abducted and brought here against your will. The bare facts would look bad in a court, and I've no wish to spend the rest of my life in gaol.'

'But I've told you, I wouldn't say anything to anyone. You have my word.'

His mouth twisted into an ugly parody of a smile. 'I've had plenty of opportunity to find out what a woman's word is worth. No, you'll stay here for at least a couple of weeks. You'll be treated as an honoured guest, but I'll make sure I have enough witnesses who've seen you enjoying your 'holiday' here so that even if you did go to the police afterwards, it would be just your word against mine that you didn't come here willingly.' His expression softened momentarily. 'Is it such a terrible prospect, Shandy? You planned a painting holiday, after all. Why not paint here?—in comfort instead of in some squalid shack by a river. You'll have the freedom of Chedoona, I promise.'

'But not the freedom to leave when I choose?'

'I'm sorry, no. That I can't allow you for the moment.'

Desperately, she groped for a way out. 'Jordan's expecting me at Melrose.'

'You'll have to do better than that. You said yourself that people come and go as they please at the colony.

When you don't show up, your friends will simply think you've changed your mind—won't they?'

Her voice dropped to a whisper of despair. 'Yes.' There was no-one else to wonder where she was. Even Barbara wouldn't have worried when she came out of the boutique and found Shandy gone. She would just think the tram had come along. She's probably sulking because I didn't say goodbye, Shandy thought bitterly. She felt trapped, and her misery turned to helpless rage against him. How could she have been taken in by his charm? Della had been right, he was a tyrant. 'I should have known what to expect from someone like you,' she threw at him.

He was unperturbed. 'What do you mean by that?'

'You have money, power—all the things I despise because of the hurt they can inflict on people, and you don't mind using them to get your own way.'

Her shot had gone home and his jaw muscles worked as he kept his anger in check. 'My money has nothing to do with this, Shandy.'

'Oh no? Only someone with your resources could keep me here against my will, like a caged animal. I suppose you get pleasure out of keeping people in your power?'

'You're talking nonsense,' he said coldly, but she could see that she had hurt him with her barbed comments. 'I don't get pleasure out of controlling anyone. I had hoped you and I could be friends.'

'Never!' she swore. 'I hate you for doing this to me, and I warn you, I'll take the first opportunity that comes along to get away.'

'Thanks for the warning,' he said levelly. 'You're over-wrought. Why don't you go to bed and think it over? All I'm really offering you is a couple of weeks to do what you intended to do anyway—paint. The scenery around here is the equal of any in the Flinders Ranges, so you won't want for subjects. I can take some time off to show you around . . .'

She tossed her head back. 'Don't trouble yourself on my account.'

He half turned away in annoyance. 'You're determined that nothing good will come of this, aren't you?'

'Well, what did you expect—that I should jump for joy over the prospect of being held prisoner?'

'Hardly. But I have a suspicion that being kept here isn't what's really bothering you.'

'Oh? Then what is, Mr Mind-Reader?'

'I think you're afraid of spending too much time with me because you don't trust yourself.'

'Now you're the one talking nonsense,' she rejoined. 'You hardly know me, so how can you possibly make a sweeping judgment like that?'

'You've been telling me so all evening.'

She stared at him in astonishment. 'What on earth are you talking about?'

'You've never heard of "body language", Shandy? It reveals your thoughts more accurately than all the words in the world. Verbally, you've been telling me how sweet and noble you are—which is the image I imagine you have of yourself. But you've been seducing me with your choice of poses from the moment we met. Whatever you tell other people—and yourself, for all I know—you're a very sexy lady, Charlotte Farrer.'

She crossed her arms protectively across her chest, and just as quickly let them drop to her sides again before he could interpret *this* pose his own way, too.

The nerve of the man! All sense of decency and restraint fled with her rising anger. 'You really do have an inflated opinion of yourself, don't you?' she demanded. 'I think you're the one who sees yourself in your pirate forbear's shoes, sweeping women off their feet. Yet you couldn't keep a wife at home and the only way you can get your daughter to visit you is to drag her here by force. Some Lothario!'

He took a step towards her, his hands balling into fists at his sides, and for a moment, she was afraid he was going to hit her. With a visible effort, he relaxed.

She clutched a hand to her mouth in horror. 'Oh God, I shouldn't have said that. I'm sorry.'

'But you did say it. So now I know what sort of image you have of me. It seems as if I was wrong about you, Shandy. At first, I thought you were different—warm and caring. But you're just like all women—heartless and cold, traitorous to your beautiful core. You don't care how your words hurt, do you?'

'I said I'm sorry.'

'You use words as a weapon when it suits you,' he went on as if she hadn't spoken, 'yet you expect me to take your word that you won't go to the police. If I had any doubts about what I was doing, you've just settled them for me. Goodnight.'

With that, he turned on his heel and left her alone. She stared after him in shock. She had never said such terrible things to anyone before. What had come over her now, to lash out like that? After all, what he was expecting of her wasn't really so unreasonable. She could paint here as well as anywhere else. And hadn't she felt a touch of regret at not being able to stay in this lovely old house for a while? Now she had the opportunity and she was acting as if he had suggested something terrible.

Was it only because he hadn't given her a choice? His words mocked her as she stood in the empty gallery which still echoed from his departing footsteps. 'You're afraid of spending too much time with me because you don't trust yourself.'

Could it possibly be true? She hadn't been conscious that her words were telling him one thing while her body said the opposite, but as an artist and a model herself, she was only too aware that the choice of pose could speak volumes. Watching him across the table at dinner, she had been more aware of him than she had ever been of any man before, despite the difference in their ages. She hadn't been disturbed by his wealth then. Yet there was no denying, it was the one thing which gave him power over other people. Without it, he wouldn't be able to manipulate her as he was doing.

She experienced a wave of the same sick feeling which had swept over her when she was given the news of her parents' death. It had been money which destroyed them; now it was being used as a weapon against her. Was great wealth always such a monstrous, evil influence?

It seemed so. She thought longingly of the colony in the Flinders Ranges. Most of the artists who went there were poor and struggling, but at least they were honest, not treacherous and manipulating like Russell Stratton. He must have been planning to keep her here from the first, using his charm and flattery to distract her from what he had in mind.

He must have misread the message her body was giving him—there was no chance she would fall for him. She was too aware of the evil inherent in his wealth and power. A buccaneer he might be, and she couldn't deny that she found him attractive. But she would have to resist it if she wasn't to be destroyed by him.

CHAPTER THREE

AFTER last night's confrontation, Shandy had been sure she would toss and turn all night, but she must have been more tired than she allowed for, because she fell asleep as soon as her head touched the feather pillow. The next thing she knew, the sun was streaming across the room, painting the lovely antique furniture with golden highlights.

Half awake, she looked around, orienting herself. Then it came back. She was a prisoner here! Try as she might to tell herself she was being melodramatic, she couldn't take any pleasure from the idea of spending the next couple of weeks at Chedoona Downs, under such conditions.

How different it would have been if she was really an honoured guest, instead of just in name. She would have taken a real delight in the century-old farmhouse with its marvellous collection of paintings and superb old furnishings. Beyond the property, the rocky coastline with its towering craggy cliffs would have challenged her to try to capture their grandeur on paper.

'Think about it,' Russell had urged. Last night she had been much too tired. Did the situation look any more appealing now she was refreshed after a good night's sleep? It was hard to see how it could. She was still being kept here against her will, at the mercy of Russell Stratton and his open chequebook with which he could buy and sell people as easily as he did his crops and machinery.

Thinking about Russell reminded her of his disturbing comment in the gallery last night. It was absurd to suggest that she could be attracted to him in . . . in that way. She wasn't interested in *any* man, not until she met the one who would ultimately be her husband. She had certainly never indulged in any of the sexual adventures the other girls she knew found so intriguing. The students at the modelling academy talked as if they were in and out of bed with different men all the time. Why was she always the only one who considered such behaviour unacceptable?

'You're scared,' came the unwilling response from deep inside her. 'You're afraid Russell was right—that you are a . . . how did he put it? . . . a sexy lady, and if you weaken even a little, you won't be able to live up to those high-sounding ideals you've always been so proud of.'

Appalled at her own thoughts, she sat up in bed and was about to jump out when the door was opened cautiously.

Helen Crossley put her head around the door. 'Good, you're awake. Mr Stratton said not to disturb you since you'd had a long day yesterday, but I thought you might like some tea and toast.'

Over Shandy's half-hearted opposition, Helen placed a bed tray across her knees and poured a cup of fragrant tea, then stood by while Shandy took a sip.

'That's lovely, thank you,' she said, since the housekeeper was apparently waiting for her reaction.

'My pleasure, dear. I wanted to apologise about mistaking you for Barbara Stratton yesterday. You should have said something.'

So neither Russell nor Robin had explained all the details of her arrival here. 'I . . . er . . . I was coming with Barbara, but she couldn't make it, so I came alone,' she explained. There was no need to involve Mrs Crossley in the kidnapping fiasco.

'I see. Well, no harm done, then. I hope you'll enjoy your visit here, anyway. How long are you staying?'

As short a time as possible, Shandy thought. Aloud, she said, 'It's not definite. A couple of weeks at the most.' There, that was near enough to the truth.

Mrs Crossley beamed. 'That's good news. I get so little female company here that it's a pleasure to have someone I can talk fashion and cooking with. Of course, Ceduna's not far away, but I can't be bothered going back and forth, so I end up spending most of my time here.'

She opened the curtains wide, letting more of the golden sunshine stream into the room. 'Would you like another cup of tea, dear?'

'No, this is fine, thanks.'

'Good. I'll be getting on with breakfast, then. Would you like a tray brought up here?'

The tea and toast would have been more than enough to satisfy Shandy until lunchtime, but she didn't want to upset the housekeeper, who was only trying to be kind. 'Don't go to any trouble, please. I'll shower and dress and be down in a jiffy.'

'No need to hurry. Remember, you're on holiday, so take all the time you want. I'll keep your food warm till you're ready.'

'You're spoiling me!' Shandy protested, but Mrs Crossley shrugged off her protests.

'I enjoy looking after people,' she assured Shandy. 'After my Arthur died, I had no-one who needed me, until Mr Stratton offered me this job. Robin's old enough to look after himself, so it's a rare treat when I have someone new to fuss over.'

'All right, as long as you really don't mind.'

Shaking her head, Mrs Crossley bustled out, leaving Shandy alone with her thoughts.

It seemed ungrateful after Mrs Crossley's pleasure in
having her here, but she was still determined to get away,
if only to show Russell Stratton that he couldn't manipulate people to suit himself. So Ceduna wasn't very far
away. From what she knew of the area, the town had an
airport. She didn't have much money with her, but if she
could just get to Ceduna, surely a ticket to Adelaide
wouldn't be beyond her means.

Feeling much better, she sipped her tea and nibbled the
hot toast, then threw aside the covers.

Her window faced north and she looked out, curious to
see more of her surroundings. For hundreds of kilometres,
as far as the horizon, the countryside spread before her flat
and almost featureless. It was spring, so the wheatfields
were a mass of rippling gold. Beyond the cultivated land
lay arid country with only low-growing scrub and coarse
grasses, and here and there, patches of twisted eucalyptus.
She couldn't help wondering how anyone could choose to
live in such a desolate place.

She showered quickly in the bathroom adjoining her
room. As she emerged, she caught sight of the Victorian
water jug on her dresser. Not so many years ago, she
would probably be having her wash out of that, she
thought, instead of in the well-appointed bathroom which
looked as if it was a later addition to the house. The water
had a strange taste, she discovered when she brushed her
teeth. She guessed it came from underground, so it would
be minerals she could taste.

After a disdainful glance at her own clothes, she opened
the door to the built-in wardrobe. Russell had said she
could wear anything she liked, so why not do just that? Of
course, she wouldn't dream of keeping any of the clothes,
however lovely, since she couldn't accept such a personal
gift from him. But there was no harm in giving her

flagging spirits a boost by making sure she looked her best. It would show Russell Stratton that she wasn't defeated yet.

His tastes were surprisingly imaginative, she found. Many fathers, choosing clothes for a daughter, would have settled for demure little dresses with Peter Pan collars, and 'sensible' skirts and twin sets. But among the collection, she discovered a pair of designer label knicker-bocker pants in khaki, and a co-ordinating western style shirt in olive and lemon check with the subtlest hint of gold thread running through it. Her own tan leather pumps completed the outfit.

She debated whether to wear make-up, then decided that the natural look would be more in keeping with the farm surroundings, so she applied a generous layer of moisturiser to protect her skin from the sun and smoothed a moisturising lipstick over her lips, giving them a full look that didn't appear too made-up.

Satisfied, she made her way downstairs.

The dining room was shadowy and deserted, but she could hear voices coming from the wing beyond it, so she ventured towards the sound.

'Ah, there you are! Sleep well?'

'Good morning, Robin. Yes, thank you.'

He noticed the coolness in her tone. 'Still haven't forgiven me for yesterday?'

His mother looked up from setting plates on the table. 'What happened yesterday?'

'Robin and I had . . . a misunderstanding,' Shandy said firmly, and saw Robin relax a little.

'But it's all cleared up now, isn't it?' he asked.

'Let's say, I understand your motives better,' she compromised.

Mrs Crossley looked relieved. 'I'm glad. We depend so

much on each other out here that it's better not to have bad feelings between people.' She gestured towards a sideboard set with large serving dishes. 'Help yourself to breakfast, dear. There's orange juice in the jug.'

'Aren't you having any?' Shandy asked when Mrs Crossley turned to leave.

'I've already had mine. I've got chores to do, so I'll leave you two to enjoy your food.'

Robin waited until his mother had gone, then gave Shandy a grateful smile. 'Thanks for not saying anything to Mum about yesterday. She had a rough time after Dad died, and I don't want to upset her now she's finally settling down. It was pretty stupid of me to mistake you for Barbara.'

'It's over now. Russell explained everything, so there's no need to worry your mother,' she said.

'Am I forgiven then?'

'I didn't say that.'

He grinned broadly. 'You're still mad at me because I kissed you at the airport yesterday. If I hadn't you'd have gotten us all arrested.'

'Actually, I'd forgotten all about it,' she said airily, annoyed when she felt her cheeks colour. 'Tell me, do all the men at Chedoona Downs have such inflated opinions of their sex appeal?'

He winced. 'Ouch! You are touchy this morning. You make a harmless kiss sound like attempted rape.'

She looked around, anxious to change the subject. 'Is Russell joining us for breakfast?'

'No, the Boss is out with the jackeroos, checking the experimental crops. He asked me to show you around the property today, since he's tied up.'

She was unaccountably disappointed that she wouldn't be seeing him. She had a pretty good idea why he was 'tied up', remembering the fury in his eyes when she accused him of not being able to keep a wife or daughter at home, except by force. She must have been out of her mind to say such a cruel thing. Much as she disliked him and hated the way he had forced his will on her, she had no right to slander him like that. But it was too late now, the words were out. She could hardly blame him if he never spoke to her again.

This prospect depressed her, though she couldn't think why. Unhappily, she sat down at the table and poured herself a glass of orange juice.

'You'll have to eat more than that,' Robin stated. Ignoring her assurances that she wasn't hungry, he went to the sideboard and piled a plate with strips of bacon, fluffy scrambled eggs and grilled tomatoes, then set it down in front of her.

'We aren't going anywhere until you've made a dent in that,' he told her sternly.

She smiled involuntarily. 'You sound just like my mother used to. She was always holding the starving children of Asia over my head.'

'Mine too,' he said ruefully. 'You know, you should smile more often. It turns you from attractive into stunning.'

She ignored the flattery and reluctantly took a mouthful of food. At the first few bites, her appetite returned and she was surprised to look down and find that she had cleaned her plate.

'I knew you could do it,' Robin praised. 'Now I can take you on the grand tour.'

'Shouldn't we clear away the dishes first?'

'We just stack them in the kitchen. One of the jackeroos has a wife who comes in to give Mum a hand.'

Since washing dishes came a poor second to looking

around the property, she was glad to help him stack the dishes in the kitchen and leave them for someone else to wash.

Outside in the sunshine, he handed her a broad-brimmed hat. It was a typical bushman's hat in khaki, needing only the addition of a row of corks bobbing on strings around the rim to make it look like something out of a campfire yarn. 'Am I supposed to wear this?'

'It's that or sunstroke. Don't worry if it doesn't quite go with your fashionable outfit. You're the sort of girl who would look good in anything.'

'I take it that's a compliment,' she said cheekily. Despite their unfortunate beginning, she liked Robin more the longer they were together. It was a pity Russell didn't view her in such a favourable light, she thought. Not that his opinion of her mattered.

With an effort, she dismissed all thoughts of him from her mind and concentrated on what Robin was telling her.

'Chedoona Downs covers forty-six thousand hectares,' he began.

'Not all of it cultivated, surely?'

'No. Only about half is suitable for farming. The rest is too arid. I suppose Russell has told you how his family came to settle here?'

'Some of it,' she said. 'But not much about the property itself.'

'Around here we get cycles of several good years followed by bad ones. The first settlers arrived in the middle of a good spell and thought it would always be like that. So they planted crops and brought in sheep where the land was totally unsuitable. When the bad times came, they were ruined.'

'Were the Strattons among them?' she asked.

'They were lucky. Only some of Chedoona land is really

arid. That's why only half is cultivated now. We've learned enough to know there's no point even trying with the rest.'

'What happened to the unlucky ones?'

Robin shrugged. 'Many of them just walked off their land and didn't come back. That's why they call this country Heartbreak Plains.'

Shandy felt a shiver play up and down her spine. Heartbreak Plains—the name seemed like an omen. But an omen warning her against what? She didn't plan on losing her heart here, did she? She made an effort to concentrate. 'How do you cope in a drought?'

'It doesn't make things any easier, but it's part of the package,' he said philosophically. 'Some of the farmers around here are nearly bankrupt because of the current dry spell, which is one of the longest on record. Scientific farmers like Russell are better off than the ones who stick to traditional methods. Like most of the properties around here, Chedoona used to be mostly under wheat with barley on the poorer soils, and merinos and crossbreds as part of the operation.'

She thought back to the aerial view she'd gained of Chedoona when she arrived. 'I didn't see any sheep.'

'Not any more. Russell only brings them in to clean up the stubble residue from the crops. The return is as good as when they were here all the time. That's the kind of changes I meant. We're also getting better returns by rotating the seed crops in different paddocks, and putting in peas and beans as experimental crops.'

Despite her dislike of Russell as a man, she was impressed with the management of his property. Although he had inherited it, it seemed he was not content to rest on any laurels. Under his guidance, Chedoona would be even more flourishing when he handed it on to his heir. Would that ever happen? she wondered. She couldn't in her wildest dreams imagine Barbara as a farmer. Away from her bright lights and creature comforts, she would wilt like a neglected flower. 'What will happen to all this in future?' she asked Robin.

'Who knows? If Barbara Stratton doesn't want to run it, it might be broken up like many of the old land holdings have been.' He turned back towards the house, deep in thought. 'Of course, Russell could still marry again. He's got plenty of time and he has quite a reputation as a ladies' man around here. I've told Mum she could do worse.'

Russell Stratton marrying Helen Crossley? It seemed logical now she considered it. Helen was older than Russell, but she would do a splendid job of running the household, and Russell was obviously fond enough of Robin to consider him a suitable heir. To her surprise, Shandy found that this idea troubled her. She didn't quite know why, but she felt sure that Russell wouldn't be content with companionship and home comforts. She had a feeling he would want more—much more—from the woman he chose to share his life.

'You're thinking far too much about Russell Stratton,' she told herself in annoyance. What he did with his future was no concern of hers, and Robin's casual comment that he was considered a ladies' man around the district confirmed her suspicion that people were mere playthings to him, herself included.

Glad of the distraction, she climbed into the four-wheel-drive vehicle and they set off on a tour of the property. All around her the plains were flat and dry against a neatly sculptured horizon, occasionally broken by whirling windmills drawing water from bores sunk deep into the artesian basin which, Robin told her, lay beneath the land.

'It's easy to imagine this country as it was when there were no white settlers,' she said dreamily.

'Isn't it? The Eyre Peninsula must be one of the parts of Australia least changed by the white man. Of course, the saltbush has mostly been eaten out by sheep and replaced by grassland, but other than that, the fences and homesteads are too far apart to make an impact on the landscape. It's easy to imagine you're the only person out here.'

They drove in companionable silence, broken only by Robin's occasional comment on some aspect of the property. Then they heard the distant sound of motors and voices, and crested a hill to find a group of people and motor-cycles clustered in a paddock below them.

'That's Russell and the jackeroos,' Robin explained. 'Want to stretch your legs for a minute?'

She was glad he hadn't suggested they go down there, because she didn't feel ready to face Russell yet after the angry scene in the gallery last night. She climbed out of the car and was immediately enveloped in a great silence under the broad sky. The voices from below reached them as a faint murmur, and there was no other sound to break the awesome stillness.

'Impressive, isn't it?' Robin asked, sensing her reaction.

'Yes, very,' she agreed, feeling tempted to whisper.

From the back of the car, Robin produced a vacuum flask of iced lime cordial which he poured into plastic cups. He handed her one and they sipped the drinks while they watched the men working in the paddock.

'You think a lot of your boss, don't you?' she probed after a while.

'Oh yes. He did a lot for me and Mum after Dad died. Would've done a lot more if I wasn't stubborn enough to want to make my own way. Pity he had such a rough time with his marriage.'

She was tempted to ask him exactly what had gone wrong between Russell and Della. Instinctively, she knew that Robin would resent her question out of loyalty to Russell, so she held her tongue. Then she remembered why she had been so keen to accompany Robin on this inspection tour.

'Where is the nearest town from here?' she asked, keeping her tone deliberately casual.

'Ceduna's a couple of hours drive away. That's the biggest settlement on the Peninsula, but there are a few small ones.'

'Do you go to town very often?'

'Only if we need something or there's a dance on or some such. I'm going tomorrow, as it happens. Some tractor parts we've been waiting on have finally come in.'

She strove to conceal her growing elation. 'I've never been to Ceduna. Would you mind if I came in with you?'

He shifted uncomfortably from one foot to another. 'If it was up to me, I'd be delighted to have your company. But the Boss wants you to stick around here for a few days. I'm leaving pretty early anyway—driving's cooler then, so nothing'd be open in Ceduna.'

She seethed inwardly, wondering what reason Russell had given to Robin for wanting to keep her on the property. Maybe none had been needed, given Robin's loyalty to his boss. He wouldn't even question the order. Well, she wasn't giving in so easily. Russell's observation about body language had given her an idea. She sidled closer to Robin and stroked a hand along his arm. 'What harm could there be in taking me into town?' she wheedled.

Robin reddened. 'Well, er . . . none, I guess. It's just . . .'

She blessed her model's training. Monica Giles had drummed into them repeatedly how important it was to suit one's pose and movements to the occasion. Provocative poses had been a must to 'sell' expensive lingerie, for example. 'Then you will take me?' she urged, draping herself against him the way she'd been taught.

His head bent closer, and for a moment she thought he might be tempted to kiss her. 'All right,' he said throatily. 'Be out the front at six tomorrow morning.'

Carefully, she pulled away from him and leaned against the car. Then she remembered the group in the paddock and her breath caught in her throat. Unbeknown to her, they had moved closer, and now she could clearly make out Russell's face in the group. He was looking directly towards her. 'You're a very sexy lady,' he had told her last night, and now, she could swear he was saying. 'I told you so.' She was imagining it, she must be.

She forced herself to look again, but by now Russell had his back to them and was crouched down, sifting soil between his fingers, making her feel foolish for attaching so much importance to what had been only an idle glance their way.

Robin gave her a bemused look, knowing he had been out-manoeuvred but not quite sure how. 'We'd better be getting back,' he said awkwardly.

He dropped her back at the homestead and disappeared towards the machine shed, muttering something about a tractor. She felt a brief pang of guilt for putting him in such a difficult spot, but she reminded herself that he was on Russell's side—and Russell was the enemy.

Mrs Crossley was working in the kitchen when she went

inside. She thrust the blackened tins of bread into the oven, then turned to Shandy. 'Join me for a cup of tea?'

It seemed that in Mrs Crossley's book, the world ran on cups of tea, and Shandy accepted her offer gratefully. She was wondering how to fill in the rest of her day and evening before she could get away with Robin tomorrow.

Helen put a plate of freshly made scones, jam and cream in front of her, then poured their tea. 'Delicious,' Shandy enthused, taking a bite. The pastry almost melted in her mouth.

Helen beamed. 'That's what I like to see. These days, too many young girls just play with food for fear of gaining an ounce. I'm glad you're not one of those.'

Helen's reference to her as a young girl reminded Shandy of Robin's comment this morning. Somehow, the idea of Helen as the next Mrs Stratton disturbed her more than she thought it should. Why should I care? she asked herself breezily. He can marry Helen Crossley and have a dozen little heirs to Chedoona. Unwillingly, she recognised the thought as bravado.

'This is a charming kitchen,' she commented to distract herself. 'Is it the original one?'

'Goodness, no,' Helen replied. 'In those days there was a drip safe and a colonial brick oven—like the large oven of a wood stove but built into a fireplace with the open fire on top. This is much more modern, built when Mr Stratton brought his bride home. He had the men's dining room and the original kitchen combined into this big one, and added a pantry and coolroom. A new men's dining room has been built onto the jackeroos' quarters at the back, beside a new meat room.'

Shandy hardly heard most of this. She was assailed by a disturbing vision of Russell carrying his bride over the stone threshold of Chedoona Downs. Thinking of Della now, so cool and sophisticated, it was hard to imagine her at home in these surroundings. 'Did you know Della Stratton very well?' she asked.

Helen frowned. 'Well enough, I'm afraid. Stuck-up madam she was too. Nothing was good enough for her, including her neighbours. We tried to do the right thing, welcoming her into the community, but she was always putting the country down. Everything was better in the city.'

'Then she didn't come from around here?'

'Not her. Her family only moved here when her father became the local bank manager.'

Money again, Shandy thought disconsolately. She could imagine Russell as a customer of the bank, being steered towards the manager's eligible daughter. Della was still a lovely woman, so it wasn't hard to picture how dazzling she must have looked as a teenager.

'What went wrong between Della and Russell?'

Helen looked uncomfortable. 'It's old news, dear. More tea?'

'No thanks. I have some things to do in my room.'

'All right. If you'd like a swim later, there's a pool out at the back you can use.'

A swim sounded like heaven right now, but first she had to organise her packing for tomorrow. She couldn't very well take her suitcases with her. They would make it too obvious that she didn't plan to return with Robin. If he knew that, he would refuse to take her along, and she was determined to get to Ceduna tomorrow.

She studied her luggage thoughtfully. In one case, she had packed a roomy canvas holdall, intending to use it to carry her painting things when she went off for a day in the ranges. She unpacked it and managed to cram half her clothing into it, as well as her make-up and purse. Regretfully, she would have to leave her painting supplies behind, but she could send for them once she was safely back in Adelaide. To camouflage the things in the holdall, she placed her sketch pad and a supply of pencils on top. She would tell Robin that she needed the gear to do some sketching while she waited for him in Ceduna.

Her swimsuit caught her eye and she remembered Helen's reference to a pool. It was an unexpected luxury in such dry country, and she decided to investigate it. She had packed the bikini in case she wanted to cool off in the creek beside the artists' colony, and she slipped into it now, then slid her feet into rubber thongs and hurried downstairs.

The pool turned out to be a converted rainwater tank. Its walls had been sunk into the ground and landscaped to blend with the surroundings. Somehow, it looked more appropriate than a modern tiled pool would have done. The water was blissfully cool and, surprisingly, chlorinated, serviced by a modern filter and pump mechanism she could hear humming away among the shrubbery.

After her swim she lay on a shaded patch of grass and let her thoughts wander. The place seemed almost deserted and the silence was broken only by the pump and the steady hum of insects. She hadn't seen Robin since they parted this morning, but she had heard the sound of a motorbike engine starting up, suggesting that he had gone off somewhere, probably to join Russell and the others.

How much had Russell seen of her behaviour with Robin? From where he was, he would have seen them standing close together, and Robin's head bend down towards hers. Would he think they had kissed? It could have seemed like it from afar.

Well, what of it? He might own his employees in body but surely not in soul. She knew Robin was attracted to

her, and it bothered her that she had used this attraction
to get her own way. Russell would find out the truth soon
enough, when she had gone. Until then, let him think she
was interested in Robin. It would give the lie to Russell's
fantastic idea that she was attracted to him.

Restlessly, she went back to her room and dressed, her
jeans and shirt feeling sticky and uncomfortable after the
freedom of her bikini. She wandered listlessly around the
house for a while until she found herself back in the
gallery. She was tempted to fetch her sketch block and
practise sketching some of the scenes in the paintings, but
the gallery reminded her too much of her quarrel with
Russell. She went back to her room and browsed through
the bookshelves there until she found something to read.

She became so absorbed in a book about the history of
the Eyre Peninsula that she hardly noticed the time
passing until Helen Crossley knocked on her door. 'Din-
nertime,' she called.

'I lost track of the time. Is it all right if I come down
dressed as I am?'

'Of course. Mr Stratton's lecturing at the Agricultural
College tonight, so I was going to ask if you'd rather have
dinner in the family room with Robin and me.'

If Shandy was disappointed that Russell wouldn't be
joining them, she was careful to hide it. 'I'd like that,' she
said.

The Crossleys were pleasant company, but Robin was
strangely withdrawn all through the meal, and afterwards
when they sat drinking their coffee on the airy front
verandah. Shandy wondered if he was regretting his
decision to take her into town with him. She hoped he
wouldn't get into any trouble because of it, and resolved to
call Russell once she was safely away, to assure him that
the idea had been hers alone.

It was a relief when Robin and his mother said their goodnights and went home to their quarters adjacent to the main house, allowing her to retire to her own room.

With no alarm clock to rouse her, she was afraid of missing her rendezvous with Robin, so she spent a restless night during which she kept waking up every few minutes to check on the time. As well, her dreams were haunted by a tall ship manned by a Greek pirate who kept her aboard his ship and refused to let her off.

'Let me go! Let me go!' she screamed aloud, waking herself. Startled, she sat up in bed and groped for her watch. The luminous dial told her it was a quarter past five—time to get up and get ready.

As quietly as she could, she dressed, afraid of waking Russell. No-one stirred as she took her holdall and tiptoed down the staircase to the kitchen.

The fear of waking anyone prevented her from cooking herself any breakfast, so she settled for a glass of orange juice and a cold chicken drumstick she found in the refrigerator.

At five to six, she tidied away the remains of her picnic and went outside to wait for Robin. The air was cool and crisp with a dawn freshness and was filled with the morning calls of birds. She took a deep breath. Soon she would be free.

Promptly at six, the Range Rover appeared and Robin pulled up in the shade of a eucalyptus tree. Why didn't he drive closer to the front door? she wondered, then realised that he was probably afraid of waking the household, too.

She hurried to the car and Robin leaned across to open her door from the inside. He was wearing the same broad-brimmed style of hat he had loaned her yesterday, and his features were deeply shadowed.

With a sigh of relief, she climbed in beside him and

slammed the door shut, then turned to thank him for giving her the lift. 'I'm looking forward to seeing Ceduna,' she told him. Especially the airport, she added to herself.

Without responding he started the engine and began to drive off, only then turning towards her. 'I'm glad to be of service.'

In shock, she whirled towards him, hampered by the seatbelt fastened across her chest. 'You!' she gasped.

They emerged into sunlight then, and she could see what should have been obvious before. The broad set of the shoulders, the chiselled features under the hat, should all have forewarned her that her driver was not Robin Crossley, but Russell himself.

CHAPTER FOUR

'YES, it's me,' he said sardonically, enjoying her stunned reaction.

At once, she reached for the door handle, but he slammed his foot on to the accelerator and the car shot away from the homestead in a flurry of dust. Furiously, she flung herself back against the upholstery. 'You're very fond of carrying me off in cars, aren't you?' she ground out.

He shook his head. 'You can't blame me this time. You got in of your own accord, remember?'

'I wouldn't have done so if I'd realised you were driving. I suppose you ordered Robin not to show up.'

His eyes flattened and the teasing smile faded. 'Robin believes you're staying here to have a much-needed rest. He was concerned that the trip to town wouldn't be good for you, so he came and checked with me. Which was as it should be—my staff are very loyal.'

'Browbeaten, more likely,' she seethed. Now she understood why Robin had been so quiet during dinner last night. He had known he would not be able to comply with her request, and hadn't wanted to break the news to her. Damn them all for conspiring against her!

At the same time, she felt a twinge of remorse. She *had* put Robin in a difficult position. Russell was his boss, so it was hardly surprising if he placed Russell's opinion ahead of hers. Still, she was not going to let Russell get away with this so easily. 'You just can't resist throwing your weight around, can you?'

He shrugged. 'Have it your own way. You seem determined to cast me in the role of power-mad capitalist, so go right ahead. But I wouldn't waste your time trying to seduce young Robin, if I were you.'

'But I wasn't . . .' she tailed off in dismay. He *had* seen her flirting with Robin on the ridge. He was not to know it had been a deliberate attempt to get her own way.

'I'm glad you aren't going to add blatant lies to everything else,' he said, noting her chastened expression. 'Yes, I saw how you behaved on the property yesterday. You deliberately enticed Rob to kiss you, so it was hardly surprising when he complied so enthusiastically. But I should warn you that he has a fiancée—a nurse at Ceduna Hospital. If you do anything to damage that relationship . . .'

'You must be a . . . a power-mad capitalist,' she interrupted vehemently, 'if you think I'm as callous as that. I wouldn't think of coming between Robin and his fiancée. I didn't know he had one.'

'Well, now you do,' he said evenly.

'You don't trust me at all, do you?' she said sourly.

'I've told you, I don't trust any woman. You're all two-faced when everything's said and done. It's just as well that you knew in advance that Robin isn't my heir or I'd suspect you of doing a little fortune-hunting while you're here.'

'You're unbelievable!' she gasped.

'No, just a realist. Your behaviour today has shown me just how far I can trust you.'

The wheatfields stretching on either side of the car limited her view of the surrounding countryside. 'Where are you taking me?' she demanded.

'You wanted to see Ceduna, and see it you shall. Then you'll be coming back with me to Chedoona Downs—

which wasn't what you planned to do, was it?'

Gazing out of the window, although there was nothing to see, she kept her face averted. 'More of your "body language"?'

'Not this time.' Reluctantly, she swivelled around. His eye was on the over-full bag at her feet.

'You weren't very discreet about your intentions, were you?'

She clenched her hands in her lap, fighting an overwhelming temptation to beat the self-satisfied expression off his face with her fists. He was easily the most arrogant, self-opinionated man she had ever met!

He was rich and powerful and he thought that justified anything he chose to do. He probably couldn't stand the thought of any woman being immune to his wealth and charms.

Well, he'd better get used to it. 'Take me back to Chedoona Downs,' she ordered.

He quirked an eyebrow upwards. 'I thought you couldn't wait to get away from the place.'

'I can't, don't get me wrong,' she assured him, tossing her head defiantly, 'but I don't wish to spend any more time in your company than I must. I'd prefer to wait out the rest of my sentence in my room at Chedoona.'

He laughed explosively and the rich sound ricocheted around the enclosed cabin, drowning the soft whisper of the car's air conditioner. 'Are you going to insist on rations of bread and water, too?'

She stared at him. It was only the second time in their short acquaintance that she had heard him laugh in genuine amusement, without mockery or derision, and the effect was extraordinary. His face took on an almost boyish appeal. The harsh planes and angles softened dramatically and his eyes glinted with devilish pinpoints of light.

His laughter was so infectious that she giggled back. After all, the idea of her beautiful bedroom as a cell was as absurd as comparing Helen Crossley's gourmet cooking with prison fare. Her giggles turned to helpless laughter, and soon both of them were laughing uproariously as they bowled along the deserted road.

'Oh, stop, please s-stop it,' she begged, feeling tears spill from the corners of her eyes. She gripped her aching sides.

He brought the vehicle to a smooth halt at the roadside and turned to look at her. Gradually, her laughter subsided as he waited, watching her.

'What's the matter?' she asked self-consciously when he continued to appraise her silently.

He reached up and grazed her cheek with the back of his hand. His touch was a curious blend of velvet skin and fine dark hairs which teased her face. 'Nothing's the matter,' he said at long last. 'You're beautiful when you laugh, did you know that?'

The air conditioner was no match for the heat that welled up from within her. 'You're teasing me,' she said huskily.

'If I was, you'd know it. No—with that hectic colour in your cheeks and your eyes afire, you're quite breath-taking.'

Now she was sure he was teasing her. As soon as they stopped, dust as fine as talcum powder had seeped into every crevice to coat her hair and clothes, and she could feel a river of perspiration wending its way down her back. How could he find her beautiful when she looked like a grubby child?'

Nevertheless, the air between them was charged with a

sensation like electricity. She leaned towards him as if drawn by a magnet. He responded from his side until their heads were almost touching, and she felt the soft wind of his breath on her face. Instinctively, she parted her lips and tilted her face upwards, her eyes transfixed by his gaze. An aching sense of longing, of incompleteness, gripped her and she was aware of a hunger she knew no food could satisfy. Russell was going to kiss her, and the crazy part was, she wanted him to do it more than she had ever wanted anything in her life before.

Just when she thought his lips were certain to claim hers, he groaned aloud and wrenched himself back to his own side of the car. Bewildered, she watched as he slammed the car into gear and swung it back onto the road with an aggressiveness which sent the tires spinning in the dust.

What had gone wrong? Had he been leading her on all the time just to prove to her that he could? Oh God, she had fallen so neatly into his trap. Despite all her stupid protests and moralising to herself, he had demonstrated how easily he could overpower her, while she sat there, hungering for the taste of his kiss and quivering with desire. For although she lacked experience, she instinctively recognised the sensation he had aroused in her.

She knew she should feel reprieved, but instead, she felt cheated, the ache inside remaining as a reminder of an unfulfilled promise. 'I suppose you're happy now?' she flung at him.

His anger was almost tangible. 'Happy? Whatever for?'

'You wanted to prove to me how powerful you are. Isn't that why you let me think that you . . . that you . . .'

'. . . were going to kiss you?' he finished for her. 'Yes, I was, but not to prove anything. If I'd wanted to do that, you'd be lying on the back seat with me now, instead of getting off so lightly.'

'G-getting off? I d-don't understand.'

'That's just it,' he said cryptically. 'You don't. In a few years' time when you've grown up, maybe you will.'

He was a cruel, heartless beast, she thought with renewed vigour, withdrawing into the opposite corner of the seat as far away from him as she could get. He was talking in riddles.

What did it matter anyway? He had made his point, at the same time proving to her how thin was her veneer of respectability. She had thought herself above the sexual adventuring of her friends at the Academy. But she was every bit as weak as they were, betrayed by her own body at the first opportunity. She had been strong only because her conviction had never really been tested before. Now it had, for she knew that if Russell had moved to close the space between them, she would have given in. He could have had his fill of her lips and . . . she dared not think what might have happened after that.

But was this discovery the *only* thing making her miserable? Or was her conscience troubled because she had *wanted* Russell's kiss and been cheated of it? Confused, she huddled in her seat, avoiding his gaze by pretending rapt interest in the passing scenery.

The flat wheatlands gave way to coastal plains sparsely covered with blue-green spinifex and mallee scrub. There were no homesteads in sight, and only thin strands of wire fencing gave a clue to the presence of other human beings. The lingering drought had reduced much of the topsoil to fine dust which had blown off the road surface altogether, leaving it bare, corrugated and rock-hard. Even through the excellent springing of the luxurious vehicle, she could feel the undulations in the road. At first, she tried to brace herself against the jolts, but soon learned that riding with them was a more effective way to keep her teeth from being shaken out of her head.

After a few miles of tense silence, she risked a sidelong glance at Russell. He was wholly absorbed in negotiating the rocky terrain and seemed to have forgotten her presence altogether. His hands were relaxed on the steering wheel and his gaze was fixed on the distance. He appeared to be having no trouble coping with the jolts, riding them easily—the way he would ride out all the jolts in his life, she imagined.

What would it take to throw him off stride? Apparently not the temptation to kiss her, she thought, chagrined. From his tranquil expression, she must be the only one agonising over what had nearly happened between them. Couldn't he see that it had changed everything? She couldn't stay here now, knowing how vulnerable she was. Next time, he might not be strong enough to keep himself in check—and, much as she loathed herself for it, she knew she was too weak to stop him. She would have to make him see that the best thing—the only thing—for both of them, was to let her go.

She was relieved when they finally drove off the property and onto the sealed Eyre Highway which led to the coast and the town of Ceduna.

Her first impression when they entered the seaside town was that everything was new. The limestone streets were broad and neat, decked out with trees. The buildings were mostly small and low and, if architecturally plain, were generally contemporary in style. The only buildings which seemed to be of any age were two handsome churches flanking the main street.

It came as a surprise when Russell broke into her

thoughts with the information that Ceduna had almost a century of history behind it.

'Why Ceduna and Chedoona?' she pondered aloud as the similarity between the names of the town and Russell's property occurred to her for the first time.

'Chedoona is the aboriginal name for this area,' he told her. 'It's thought to mean "a place to sit down and rest by a fresh water soakage". Over the years, the town name has been modified to Ceduna, but we retained the old name for the property. It seemed appropriate since we were among the first settlers on the Peninsula.' He gestured down a side street lined with well-spaced, handsome brick houses. 'My great-grandfather bought one of the first blocks of land in that street, just after the town was surveyed in 1900. It cost him five pounds seven shillings.'

In spite of her reluctance to be with Russell, she was intrigued by the frontier atmosphere of the town. Her fingers itched for a pencil to capture some of the scenes on paper so that she could translate them into watercolours later.

He parked the car outside a white stone building that sported a red and white striped awning under which were plastic tables and chairs placed to take advantage of the view across the bay.

'Do you have some business to do here?' she queried, her nostrils tantalised by the smell of percolating coffee that came from the café.

'You could say that. I plan to have breakfast here. I don't suppose you stopped to have any before you sneaked . . . er, left the house?'

She flushed guiltily, remembering how she had tiptoed around the kitchen this morning, fearful of waking Russell, not knowing that he was already out and about. 'I ate something,' she said defensively.

'I can guess. Fruit juice and toast.'

'Chicken drumstick,' she contradicted and was rewarded by a flash of warm smile, quickly masked.

'In that case, you won't mind joining me.'

She was hungry and the aromas coming from the café weren't helping. As she hesitated, hunger overcame all other considerations, so she slid out of the car and joined him on the kerb.

The proprietress knew him well and hurried out with a pot of freshly brewed coffee as soon as they sat down at one of the outdoor tables.

''Morning, Boss,' she beamed, 'you're bright and early.'

''Morning, Peggy. This is my . . . house guest, Shandy Farrer. Shandy, meet Peggy Holden, the best cook in Ceduna.'

'Cut it out! He just says that so I'll give him bigger helpings,' Peggy assured Shandy with a wink. 'Pleased to meet you. I hope you enjoy your visit.'

'I'm sure I will,' Shandy agreed. Strangely, she found she meant it. Her first glimpse of Ceduna had excited her and she looked forward to getting it down on paper.

After taking their orders, Peggy returned to her kitchen, leaving them to enjoy their coffee and the spectacular view.

'Sitting by the sea like this, it's hard to accept that just a few miles inland, the country's in the grip of a drought,' she marvelled.

He nodded. 'We have the best of both worlds here. Civilisation when you feel the need, and the solitude of the outback the rest of the time.'

His mention of the outback reminded her that she couldn't risk spending any more time on his property. Awkwardly, she twirled her spoon in the creamy coffee, the swirling patterns matching her confused thoughts. 'I wanted to talk to you about Chedoona,' she began.

'What about it?'

'I . . . I can't stay there any longer after what happened this morning.'

His face remained impassive. 'Oh? And just what "happened", as you put it?'

She dropped the spoon into the saucer with a clatter. 'You know perfectly well what I mean! You're a man and I'm a woman, and . . . and . . .' she tailed off, blushing furiously.

'I'm glad to see you've finally realised that,' he said drily. 'But it doesn't alter the reason why I want you to stay.' He emphasised the word, reminding her that he usually got what he wanted. 'Bringing you here will help establish that you're on holiday, not the poor unfortunate victim of a kidnapping.'

So that was why he hadn't tried to stop her coming to Ceduna. He'd deliberately introduced her to Peggy Holden as his house guest, to strengthen his story that she was here willingly. She had played right into his hands by agreeing with Peggy that she was sure she would enjoy her 'visit'. It was as well he'd forewarned her, otherwise she would have spent a happy day sketching and sightseeing, unaware that she was doing exactly what he wanted.

'I wonder how long your alibi will hold up when everyone sees you dragging me from place to place,' she sneered. 'Now I know what you're up to, I have no intention of co-operating.'

'What a pity,' he said, unperturbed. 'There's a lot to see around here, and it won't be much fun sightseeing from a locked car in this heat.'

'I'll scream the place down,' she warned.

'Then I'd have to silence your screams,' he countered,

his eyes travelling to her lips to emphasise what he had in mind. 'Come to think of it, I might enjoy myself more that way than squiring you around the sights. If I parked in the local Lover's Lane, we wouldn't even rate a passing glance.'

'You're not just a power-mad capitalist, you're a . . . a sex-fiend!' she said triumphantly.

She half-rose from the table, intending to run as far away from him as possible, but he anticipated her move and clamped a hand over her wrist. 'Sit down,' he ordered in an undertone which brooked no argument.

Sullenly, she sat down again just as Peggy returned with their food. The plates were piled with thick slabs of country bacon and golden-yolked eggs, but the food had lost its appeal. She thanked Peggy but made no move to pick up her knife and fork.

'I suggest you eat your breakfast,' he said quietly, 'We'll have a late lunch in Thevenard, but I don't plan to stop again until we get back to Chedoona tonight, and you'll be mighty hungry by then.'

'You plan, you want . . . that's all that matters, isn't it?' she said miserably. 'You don't care what I want . . . or about anybody else, do you?'

'You're acting like a child! Perhaps it was Providence that sent you to me, Shandy, because, by God, you need a man to straighten you out.'

'If by that, you mean take me to bed, it's not the answer to everything, you know!' She knew she was shouting, but was so incensed by his high-handed attitude that she didn't care who heard her.

'You're the one who keeps bringing the subject up,' he reminded her. 'But that wasn't the sort of straightening out I had in mind. Because of your parents, you have this crazy idea that money is the root of all evil, and I mean to convince you otherwise—somebody has to, for your own sake.'

'You can try all you like, but it won't change what I know to be true,' she persisted stubbornly.

'Does that mean you'll behave yourself today?'

'I don't have any choice, do I?'

'No, none.' He signalled the end of the discussion by tucking into his breakfast with every appearance of enthusiasm. After a moment's hesitation, she did the same. Refusing to eat *was* childish and would hurt no-one but herself. Besides, she had plans of her own. When he asked whether she would behave, she had evaded a direct answer. She *would* behave, but only until he was tied up with whatever business had brought him into town. Then she would slip away and find a taxi to take her to the airport and freedom.

Even in this, he had second-guessed her, as she found when they left the café and walked along the seafront reserve. 'Do you mind amusing yourself for a while until I've been to the bank, and picked up Robin's tractor parts?' he asked.

She assumed an expression of seraphic innocence. 'Of course not. I can do some sketching until you get back.'

They walked back to the car and he opened the passenger door, but before she could remove her bag, he reached in and took out the sketch book and pencils, handing them to her. 'This is all you'll need, I think.'

'My purse . . .' she began.

'Oh, you won't need that. I'll only be an hour, so if you want to do any shopping, I'll take you when I get back.'

The brute! He had effectively prevented her escaping by making sure she had no money or possessions with her.

He must have guessed what she had in mind. With a sigh of resignation, she stepped away from the car. 'Have it your way.'

He grinned, sensing her impotent fury. 'I always do.'

With that, he closed the car doors and drove off, leaving her silently raining curses on his head. When the lightning bolt she called down failed to strike his car and turn it into a smouldering ruin, she gave up and turned towards the seafront. Sulking for any length of time was foreign to her nature, so she decided to get on with some sketching, since it was the only choice she had.

At least she could show him that she had real talent, even if he didn't think much of her otherwise. 'Yes, I'll show him!' she muttered mutinously, and wandered along the reserve in search of suitable subjects.

With so many choices available, this was a difficult decision. Broad green lawns led all the way to the shores of Murat Bay, with bushy Aleppo pines at the northern end creating an interesting contrast to the straight-trunked Norfolk Island pines opposite the hotel. The reserve looked out across the bay, which was a lake-like stretch of water sheltered along the southern side by the bulk of a long island. In the distance, another settlement formed the eastern arm of the bay.

Everywhere she looked, the scenery tempted her artist's eye. But she finally succumbed to the sight of a group of fishermen dangling nets and lines off the town jetty. One old man in particular attracted her attention as he pulled in huge crabs in a wicker basket contraption. She asked whether he minded her sketching him and was rewarded by a toothless smile. 'Sketch away, lass, if you think I'm worth it, but I'm no "Blue Boy".'

Later, examining the finished sketch of the old man, she knew it was one of the best things she had ever done. She could hardly wait to get back to Chedoona and translate it into watercolours.

Since she still had a little time, she did some rough sketches of the bay from the launching ramp, looking towards the settlement in the distance. She would have to ask Russell what it was. Her final sketch was of the broad main street of Ceduna, with the Norfolk Island pines growing along the median strip as the focus. She was just putting the finishing touches to this when she became aware that someone was watching her.

Russell was looking critically over her shoulder. 'You're very good,' he said warmly.

Inexplicably, she glowed at his praise, then remembered how he had tricked her by driving off with her purse. 'I'm glad you think I'm good for something,' she retorted.

His eye travelled over her long legs stretched out in front of her, the jeans rolled to the knee for coolness. 'I'm sure you're good for a lot of things,' he said softly.

His appraisal disturbed her, although, as a model, she should have been accustomed to stares. Russell's blatant gaze was somehow different, perhaps because she couldn't just disappear down a catwalk after the parade. 'Have you finished your business?' she asked, hoping to distract him.

Well aware of her strategy, he finished his leisurely perusal of her body, then nodded. 'That's it for the day. The rest of my time's my own.'

'Won't Robin be waiting for the tractor parts?'

'There are three tractors at Chedoona—he can use one of the other two. I have other plans for today.'

She jumped up, thinking of his threat about Lover's Lane. 'What . . . what plans?'

'You'll see. Did you want to do any shopping here?'

Since she hadn't brought much money to begin with,

and she wanted to keep what little she had in case the chance of escape presented itself, she shook her head. 'No thanks. The clothes you . . . I mean, Barbara's clothes are enough for my needs, and I don't need anything else.'

'Right. We'll be on our way then.'

On their way to where? Her interest was piqued as he drove around the shore of the bay towards the settlement she had seen from the town.

It was located on a narrow strip of land along the eastern arm of the bay. Grain silos dominated the skyline and a jetty extended far out into the water. Further around the coastline clustered a fleet of small fishing boats.

'This is Thevenard,' Russell supplied as she absorbed the scene with interest.

'It looks like a fishing port,' she observed. 'What's here that you wanted me to see?'

'My roots.'

'Your what?'

'Try not to look so surprised. I told you I had something to show you—the humble beginnings of my family.'

As she digested this, they drove slowly along the foreshore while he showed her the silos which held the grain from his and similar properties. A conveyor belt carried the grain to the holds of ships anchored alongside the jetty. On the foreshore, stacks of gypsum and salt—the port's other main cargoes—glistened in the midday sun.

The area was so Greek in character that Shandy found it hard to believe it was part of Australia. The shape, colour, and names on the fishing boats; the sand and the jetty, and the little stone cottages were all unmistakably Mediterranean. Again, she felt the urge to capture its uniqueness on paper.

'What a delightful place,' she said sincerely.

'Those are the real descendants of Adonis, the pirate,' he told her, and pointed out a group of stocky, dark-skinned men in thigh-high rubber boots, with heavy jumpers tied loosely around their shoulders. He stopped the car near the men who were busy mending nets. 'Come and meet the family.'

She followed him down to the sand and was surprised to be greeted in broad Australian accents. What did you expect, broken English? Russell's glance plainly asked as she tried unsuccessfully to conceal her reaction.

She returned the greetings politely, then stood awkwardly by while Russell and the men exchanged news. It was obvious that he was a frequent and popular visitor to Thevenard. At last, one of the men stood up. 'Come back and have some coffee with us. Anna will want to meet your *felinada*.'

He looked straight at her as he said the Greek word and she wondered what it meant, and why Russell's smile suddenly widened. She resolved to quiz him about it later.

Anna was a cousin of Russell's as, it seemed, was half of Thevenard. Russell hugged her unselfconsciously, and did the same for the men in the group, then introduced Shandy around. Some of the names were Greek, others, like Russell's, were Australian.

When Anna heard that they planned to have lunch in Thevenard, she wouldn't hear of their going to a restaurant. She insisted on setting a table with freshly caught whiting, green salad, olives, cheese, and bread still warm from the oven, washed down with a flask of fruity white wine.

During lunch, the conversation took place mostly in Greek, reminding Shandy of the two worlds the family inhabited. She raised an eyebrow when she discovered that Russell was fluent in the language. After fixing him firmly in her mind as a tyrant who thought money was the key to everything, she was surprised to see how much at home he was in this simple household.

Suddenly, the number of glances her way increased, and although she couldn't understand what was being said, she realised they were discussing her. Her only consolation was the air of approval their words conveyed. At least Russell couldn't accuse her of making a bad impression.

After a while, Anna took pity on her and came to sit beside her, offering her more of the treacly coffee from a very old brass pot. 'I believe you are an artist—how clever,' she remarked.

'I'm still learning, and I can't earn a living at it,' Shandy responded.

'Oh, but to be able to express yourself in pictures at all—I wish I could do that.' She sipped her coffee thoughtfully, then set the cup down. 'Have you known Russell long?'

What had he told them about her, she wondered, not wanting to contradict him in front of his family. 'I'm a friend of his daughter's,' she compromised. Wanting desperately to get onto safer ground, she asked, 'Are you all descended from the one man?'

Anna laughed. 'I see that Russell's told you about our infamous family pirate, Adonis. His grandson, Spiros, was the real founder of Chedoona Downs, although the Strattons had been squatters on the land before that. Spiros had a son, Theo—my grandfather—who left the land to return to the sea.'

'He was the artist?' Shandy asked, remembering the paintings in Russell's collection.

'He had the gift, but he did not pursue it. He was too

anxious to be out in his boat. To him, every minute away from the sea was wasted.' She sighed. 'I wish I had inherited his talent.'

'Perhaps you did,' Shandy suggested. 'Have you ever seriously tried to paint?'

'Oh no, cooking and sewing are art enough for me. Besides, I wouldn't know where to start.'

'I could show you a few of the basics,' Shandy offered, surprising herself.

Anna's eyes shone. 'That would be splendid. But I couldn't put you to the trouble.'

'What trouble?' Russell asked, coming over to them.

'Your *felinada* said she would show me how to paint some time,' Anna enthused.

Russell frowned. 'That's very kind of her, I'm sure. But she won't really be here long enough for that. You're here to rest, remember, Shandy?'

Anna put a hand to her mouth. 'You have been ill?'

'No, Russell just fusses over me,' she said, glaring at him.

When he took her elbow and urged her to her feet, she resisted the temptation to shake off his hand. She didn't want to offend Anna's family, who had been so welcoming. 'It's time we were getting back.'

Once again, hugs were exchanged between men and women alike. When Russell reached Anna, Shandy noticed him placing an envelope into the woman's hands. Anna shook her head and tried to give it back, but he said something to her in Greek and she smiled, giving in gracefully.

They drove off to a chorus of Greek and Australian farewells. 'What was that word they called me?' Shandy asked.

'*Felinada*? It means girlfriend.'

'Girlfriend!' she exploded, 'you let them think that you and I . . . that we . . .'

'Relax,' he said mildly, 'they fully approved of you.'

As if that made it all right! She took a careful hold on her temper and decided to get her own back by needling him a little. 'I suppose you like coming here to play patron, handing out largesse?'

'No, they do all right for themselves,' he said coldly. 'But if you're wondering about the envelope, I'm putting Anna's eldest boy through Agricultural College. I don't make a big thing of it—you're the only one who knows outside the immediate family. You didn't think I had it in me, did you?'

The observation was so close to the truth that she coloured guiltily. 'They're nice people,' she said after a pause.

'That wasn't what I asked, but I can see you're not going to admit that I'm anything other than what you first decided, even after what you've seen today.'

She moved uncomfortably in her seat. It was true, the outing *had* shown her another, more human side of him, but she couldn't afford to let him know that.

Since she had no choice about remaining under his roof for the moment, her only hope of protecting herself was to keep fuelling her dislike of him.

The problem was—how long could she keep it up?

CHAPTER FIVE

THE next few days were the loneliest that Shandy could remember. The Crossleys were friendly and helpful, but remembering Russell's warning about the fiancée in Ceduna, Shandy was carefully neutral towards Robin. Most of the time he was too busy with the property to notice, but occasionally she caught him looking at her with a puzzled expression.

Staying out of Russell's way was more difficult, since he tended to seek her out. Unlike Robin, he wasn't in the least worried by her cold attitude towards him. Rather, he seemed to be amused by it until she wanted to pummel the smug expression off his face.

What did he want from her? she asked herself for the umpteenth time since their visit to Ceduna. He seemed to be waiting for something, but she had no idea what he expected of her, and she wasn't going to ask him for anything.

For her part, all she wanted from him was her freedom. She didn't like the new and totally disturbing way he had stirred her emotions. Ever since that moment in Ceduna, when he had almost kissed her, she had been aware of a feeling of dissatisfaction, as if something important was missing from her life.

In an attempt to shake off the strange feeling she threw herself into her work, completing several watercolours based on the sketches she had done at Ceduna. They were good, she observed dispassionately. But while the work satisfied her artistic needs, it did nothing to assuage the hunger that Russell had ignited inside her.

Without seeing it, she stared at the painting she was working on, and the errant thoughts assailed her again. What would it be like to be made love to by a man like Russell? To be swept into his arms and carried to his bed, there to feel him caress every part of her with possessive intimacy?

The painting swam into focus again and she shuddered. What was she thinking of? Could she conceivably have fallen in love with Russell in such a short time? Common sense told her it didn't work that way. So that left only one thing—what she was experiencing was simply a strong chemical attraction.

Perhaps it wouldn't have mattered who the man was— she might have felt the same way. He was the first man she had spent any time alone with in her adult life. The few young men she'd dated before couldn't compare with his all-pervading masculinity.

'That's all it is,' she said aloud, feeling better. Sexual attraction was very powerful, she knew despite her inexperience, but surely now she had recognised it for what it was, she would be able to control it like any other appetite. All she had to do was avoid being alone with him until she could return to Adelaide.

She had reckoned without his avowed intention to show her off around the district as his house guest, enjoying a carefree holiday.

'Get your things together,' he told her next morning after breakfast. 'We're going to Penong.'

'But I don't want . . .' she began and found his eyes on her, daring her to argue with him. She shrugged in an apparent display of resignation which she knew wouldn't fool him for a moment. 'As you wish, m'lord. What will I need?'

'A shady hat, sun-tan lotion, your swimsuit,' he reeled off, 'and don't forget your sketching things. Where we're going, you'll see some of the most spectacular scenery in Australia.'

Knowing he wouldn't stand for any delaying tactics, she hurried upstairs and collected together the items he mentioned, packing them into her holdall. She hesitated when she came to her bikini—should she leave it behind? But he was the sort of man who'd expect her to swim with or without a swimsuit, so it seemed prudent to take it.

Ten minutes later she was waiting outside when Robin drove up in the big estate car. 'Aren't we taking the four-wheel-drive?' she asked, when Robin got out and handed Russell the keys.

'Robin's using it today. Besides, I thought you'd be more comfortable in this one, with the air conditioning.'

Perversely, instead of feeling grateful, she felt cross. What did he think she was—a spoiled city girl who needed pampering? 'You didn't need to put yourself out,' she said churlishly.

'Thank you for thinking of me, Russell,' he mocked.

'I hadn't forgotten my manners,' she said coldly. 'I just don't appreciate being dragged around the district like a sideshow exhibit.'

'You aren't on exhibition today,' he assured her. 'In fact, where we're going, we'll be lucky to meet another soul.'

A warning chill played up and down her spine. 'You said we were going to Penong—isn't that a town?'

'It's a small rural community a hundred or so kilometres from here on the Nullarbor Plains.'

From her schooldays she knew that the Nullarbor was a vast, arid area bigger than the state of Victoria, mostly treeless and sparsely covered with sand, mallee scrub and a few low, stunted bushes. Its name was a corruption of the Latin for 'not any trees', which well described the hot, pitiless country where settlements of any kind were few and far between. She wasn't at all sure she wanted to venture into such territory with Russell.

As if he sensed what she was thinking, he gunned the engine and the car shot forward, giving her no chance to reconsider.

'I thought you would be pleased at the prospect of an outing,' he said as they headed towards the junction with the Highway. 'You've been spending too much time cooped up in your room. Avoiding me?'

She looked at him uneasily. Was he a mind-reader, too? 'Why should I avoid you?'

'Because I remind you of some things you'd rather not face—your femininity for one.'

'I thought you said my problem was my attitude towards money?'

'That, too. You're mixed up about a lot of things, and I'd like to help you if I can.'

The urge to lash out at him returned, and since she wasn't strong enough to do it physically, she attacked him verbally. 'Look,' she exploded, 'you may be Barbara's father but you aren't mine, and I wish you'd leave me alone.'

His face was frighteningly bland, devoid of all reaction, but his tone was cold when he responded. 'Thanks for that timely reminder. But I can assure you, my concern was anything but fatherly.'

'What do you mean?'

'I thought it was obvious when we went to Ceduna. I wanted to kiss you. In fact, I wanted to do a damned sight more than that, but I kept reminding myself that you *are* young enough to be my daughter. That's what's really bothering you, isn't it?'

'No, of course not.'

'Yes, it is. I thought you were upset because I made you accept the fact that you're a beautiful, desirable woman. But that's not the problem. You're disappointed because I backed off when I did.'

'You have a pretty high opinion of yourself if you think that!' she retorted, sounding unconvincing even to her own ears. Did she feel cheated because he had aroused her and then abandoned her? She remembered her conviction that any man would have had the same effect on her in the same circumstances, and a feeling of self-disgust overwhelmed her. How could anyone say that such a base, animal instinct was beautiful? If all humans were only victims of their body chemistry, as she now suspected she was, how could there be any such thing as love?

'You've got it wrong, you know,' he said, interrupting her thoughts.

'What?'

'You think responding to your own feelings is a weakness. But it's normal and healthy.'

She turned her head away, pretending fascination with the scenery. If she answered, she would only encourage this line of conversation.

'Have it your way,' he said softly.

Damn him! she thought fiercely. Why couldn't she be as sure of her convictions as he was of his? When she came here, she had known that it was better to be poor but happy, and had thought herself virtuous in saving herself for her future husband. She wasn't running scared, as he seemed to think. What right had he to hold her beliefs up to the light like this?

'When are you going to let me leave?' she asked, more to

distract herself than because she really cared. It didn't seem to matter any more whether she was here for another week or a month. The damage had already been done.

'Two weeks ought to do it,' he said with maddening good humour, as if he was a doctor predicting a cure instead of her gaoler pronouncing sentence. 'I brought my camera along today to get some more evidence of what a great holiday you're having.'

Indignation welled up inside her. 'If you think I'm posing for your voyeuristic photographs . . .'

'I was thinking more of candid snaps, actually, but now you've given me the idea . . .'

'You're impossible!' she seethed. A muffled sound made her turn towards him. He was laughing at her. 'Stop that,' she ordered angrily.

'Come off it, Shandy. Relax for once in your life.'

How could she relax when that would leave her vulnerable to feelings she'd rather not face? 'I don't find the situation funny,' she said primly. 'Would you, in my shoes?'

'Perhaps not,' he conceded. 'So let me put it this way. It's a beautiful day and, as an artist, you should appreciate the scenery I'm going to show you. On those grounds alone, can't we declare a truce?'

'On those grounds, I'm willing,' she agreed. It would be less wearing on her nerves than this verbal fencing.

Little by little, she did relax after that and began to enjoy the drive through wheat country which reached almost to the sea. They turned off onto a dirt road which led to a cluster of stone ruins alongside which was a cairn and plaque. 'Who was William McKenzie?' she asked as they stood looking at the memorial.

'One of the area's great pioneers,' Russell informed her.

'My great-great-grandfather, Spiros, was a contemporary of his. He was the local water diviner.'

Shandy was busy sketching the lonely ruin with its rustic wagon wheels half-hidden by tussocky grass. They and the cottage were poignant reminders of a once-thriving homestead. She looked up curiously. 'Water diviner? There's no such thing, surely?'

'Perhaps not. But I've been told that Spiros used to walk over the land holding two lengths of fencing wire in front of his chest parallel with the ground and pointing forwards like this.' He demonstrated with lengths of twig. 'When the water was nearby, the wires would quiver and swing towards the source. Where he indicated, the farmer would sink a bore and, later on, install a windmill to raise fresh water from the underground basin.'

'Did it really work?'

He shrugged. 'Who knows? I only know that Chedoona Downs is one of the best-watered properties on the Peninsula.'

She looked at him in wonder. First pirates and now water diviners! He was really the most unusual breed of man she had ever encountered.

Further west, he steered the car down a series of graded dirt roads until they were surrounded by towering sandhills. They emerged onto a deserted beach which was backed by a tangle of mangroves, creeks and cocklebeds, with the limitless ocean stretching out in front of them.

'Like to stop here for a dip?' he asked her.

The sparkling water beckoned invitingly. 'Is it safe to swim here?'

'If you don't go out of your depth. There are sharks around, so it's wise to keep a lookout, but people come from Ceduna to swim and surf here all the time.'

She needed no further invitation. Snatching her bikini

and towel from her bag, she disappeared behind a sheltering sandhill to change. Russell must have been wearing his swimming trunks under his clothes, because he was stripped and waiting at the water's edge when she emerged. Clad only in the close-fitting navy trunks, he looked more than ever like a Greek god, and she marvelled at the way his muscular body glistened in the sun.

She knew her own sleek yellow bikini flattered her figure, but for once, she wished there was a little more of it to hide her from his frankly appreciative appraisal. Her stay at Chedoona Downs had turned her golden skin to a deeper honey colour and lightened her already-fair hair, so that she looked a picture of young, vibrant good health.

As she approached the water, Russell drew a sharp breath. He half-turned towards her and seemed about to say something, then he swung back and dived cleanly into the breakers like an arrow released from a bow.

He surfaced some distance away and rolled onto his back to wave to her. 'Come on in, it's marvellous.'

She dipped a toe into the water. It was cool but welcoming after the hot sun of the plains. She dived after him but decided to swim parallel to the shore, recalling his warning about sharks. She looked around, but the only threat she could discern in the water was Russell himself. He had a lot in common with a shark, she thought as she floated lazily in the shallows. He had the same sleek, dark good looks, the same ability to attack without warning—and she had no doubt he could devour her if he chose to. She shivered although the water was far from cold. Compared with him, she was a small fish indeed.

After their swim, Shandy stretched out on her towel on the sand, and enjoyed the feel of the sun penetrating to her very bones. She had no idea what Russell was doing until he padded back across the beach, dangling something on a line. 'What's that?' she asked as droplets of water sprinkled her.

'Our lunch. Barbecued whiting.'

She watched, fascinated, as he built a small fire on the sand and cooked the fish in a cast-iron frypan he retrieved from the boot of the car. They ate with their fingers, pulling the succulent white fish off the bones with the enthusiasm of castaways.

After the meal, they washed their hands in the sea and sprawled in the lee of a sandhill to let their lunch settle. Russell had his eyes closed and Shandy studied him. Why couldn't he always be like this—safe, undemanding and fun, instead of expecting more from her than she was prepared to give?

The rest of the drive to Penong was accomplished in companionable silence as Shandy absorbed the vast emptiness of the plains around them. The highway meandered close to the coastline and there was always a little scrub and vegetation on the plains or the dunes which lay between the road and the sea.

The tiny township of Penong with its windmills; the shacks of a few desert nomads; and the huts of road-worker gangs were the only signs of human habitation. Once, Russell drew her attention to a herd of camels strung out along the horizon. Her pen flew the whole time as she tried to capture the beauty and novelty around her.

Nowhere was she more impressed than when Russell took her to the very brink of the Nullarbor Cliffs which ringed the Great Australian Bight. Until now, this part of the southern coastline had been nothing more than a curving line on a map to her. She knew she would never forget the experience of standing on the edge of the world, watching the surf crash against the towering cliffs. Forgetting her earlier objections, she even allowed Russell to photograph her against the stunning backdrop.

'Thank you for showing it to me, I'll never forget it,' she told Russell when they continued on their journey.

'I thought you'd appreciate it. I'll look forward to seeing the pictures that result from today's trip.'

It was late by the time they started back towards Chedoona Downs. Behind them, the setting sun slashed the sky with tongues of flame. Gradually, the scrub by the roadside settled into ever-deepening shadows that stirred with awakening wildlife.

'Why are we driving so slowly?' she asked Russell.

'I don't want to collect any 'roos,' he explained without taking his eyes off the roadway. 'They travel at night, and by morning, this road will be littered with them.'

'People run into them?' she asked in horror.

'You can't avoid it sometimes. They like to sit on the road, because it's warm from the sun, and they become hypnotised by car headlights. Sometimes they panic and jump the wrong way, then it's either you or the kangaroo.'

'I hope we won't have to make that choice,' she said with feeling. She couldn't bear the thought of running over one of the beautiful, sloe-eyed creatures.

They saw many kangaroos on and beside the road, and an Old Man Kangaroo kept pace with their car for a while, but, fortunately, they didn't bump into any. Shandy heaved a sigh of relief when a turn-off appeared in the headlights and she recognised the side road leading to Chedoona Downs.

'We'll be home in an hour,' Russell said as if divining her thoughts.

But luck was against them. As he slowed to negotiate a jump-up in the road, the engine sputtered and failed. He muttered an oath and reached for the starter, but there was no response. With a sigh, he climbed out and opened the bonnet.

'Is there anything I can do?' she asked, following him.

'Hold this for me.' He handed her a torch and she directed the light where he requested it, while he fiddled with the engine. She watched as he undid a lead, removed a sparkplug and held it against the metal of the engine. 'Can you start the engine for me?'

She did as she was told and heard him swear again. 'It's the electrical system,' he explained when she came back to hold the lamp again. 'There should have been a blue spark from the plug when you turned the ignition.' He went back to work and after a few minutes, straightened again. 'I've cleaned and tightened everything and checked all the terminals. The only thing left is the starter motor.'

'Is there nothing you can do?'

'Tow her back and have a new one fitted,' he said flatly.

'It's all my fault, isn't it?' she asked miserably.

In the glare of the lamp, he looked at her in surprise. 'How did you work that out?'

'If you hadn't felt the need to pamper me with a fancy, air-conditioned car, this wouldn't have happened.'

He laughed and turned her to face him. 'You silly goose. A starter motor can go at any time, without warning. Even if we'd gone out in a truck, it wouldn't necessarily have made any difference.'

'But what are we going to do?'

'Stay with the car—rule one of the outback. A car can be spotted much more easily than a person. Then we wait for Robin to come looking for us.'

'But how will he know where we are?'

'Rule two—always tell someone where you are going and when you expect to be back.'

'That's all we can do—wait?'

'Unless you feel like walking thirty kilometres in the pitch dark.'

The bush around them was full of moving, rustling shapes and the evening breeze was unexpectedly cold. She shivered. 'No, thanks. Will Robin be very long?'

Russell's hands were still on her shoulders. 'Scared to be alone with me?'

'Should I be?'

He let out a slow breath. 'Damn it, yes. But you don't know enough even for that, do you?'

She stiffened in his grasp. 'I'm not a child, you know.'

'Oh no, never that.' Abruptly he released her and rummaged about in the back of the car. A minute later, he came back with a sweater for himself and a travel rug which he draped around her shoulders.

She snuggled into it gratefully. 'I didn't know it could get so cold out here.'

'It'll get a lot colder in the next hour or so. We'd better get back into the car and close it up to retain what heat there is. Pity it had to be the electrical system, or we could have used the heater.'

He held open the rear passenger door, but she baulked. 'I'm not going in there. I'll sit in front.'

'Do you think I arranged this so I could get you into the back seat?' he growled impatiently. 'I've had a dozen opportunities today and I haven't taken advantage of one of them, now have I?'

'No, you haven't,' she agreed grudgingly.

'Then get in, for goodness' sake.'

She climbed into the car and sat hunched in one corner, as far away from him as possible. Then he startled her by pulling her towards him. 'The idea is to keep warm,' he reminded her when she tried to resist.

There was nothing for it but to move into his encircling

arm and let him draw the travel rug around them both like a cocoon. She had to admit it was warmer like that. She told herself that the heat welling up inside her was caused by the blanket and had nothing to do with his nearness, as she willed her heart to stop its frantic pounding. Robin would be here soon and everything would be all right. 'What time did you say Robin would be here?' she asked from within the cocoon.

'I didn't. I expect he'll give us an hour outside our expected arrival time before he comes looking—say three hours.'

Three hours? How could she tolerate this suffocating sensation for three hours? Never before had she been as aware of a man as she was now, cradled in Russell's arms with her head resting against his chest. She could feel his heart beating strongly through the thick sweater. He had one arm around her shoulders and the other across her lap.

'You're very tense,' he said suddenly. 'Is anything wrong?'

'No,' she said, but her voice came out as a high-pitched squeak.

'Not frightened, are you? I'm here, remember.'

As if she could forget his presence for a moment! 'I'm all right really,' she insisted, her voice sounding more natural this time. 'I think I'll try to sleep.'

Lulled by the warmth, she did manage to drift off, but her dreams were peopled by strange phantoms and nameless fears. One of her dream phantoms began to chase her and she moaned and thrashed around as she tried to get away.

'It's all right, I'm here.'

In her dream, she was aware of a hand stroking her forehead; then lips brushed her hairline so gently that she wondered if she'd imagined it. The phantom pursuer fled, and in her half-awake state, she wrapped her arms around her rescuer.

'Oh, Shandy, you don't know what you're doing to me.'

She came fully awake to find herself entwined around Russell, her legs between his thighs and her arms around his shoulders. At once she tried to extricate herself but his hold tightened. 'No, please,' she begged.

'You weren't saying that a moment ago,' he said hoarsely.

'I wasn't awake then. Now I am.'

'Good,' he murmured. Then his mouth came down on hers in a warm, possessive kiss which flooded her mind and body with sensation. His thighs tightened their grip around her legs and his mouth on hers was so demanding that she surrendered to it instinctively. Her lips parted and she tried to pull away as his tongue invaded her mouth. She had never been kissed so intimately in her life. Part of her urged her to end it now, while she still could. Still another part wanted to give in to the unbelievable sweetness.

Fireworks exploded in her brain. Distantly, she remembered that she should stop this before it got out of hand. Then she realised it was already past that point. She drew in her breath as Russell's hand found the tender flesh of her breasts and massaged them gently, sending a fever of sensations racing along her veins. She felt her nipples harden against the fabric of her shirt.

He had relinquished her mouth and was exploring her throat with his lips, making her want to moan aloud with the desire flooding through her. Impatiently, he pushed the blanket aside and continued his downward explorations, stopping only to unbutton her shirt to the waist to give him freer access to her body.

Her hands were busy too. As he claimed first one breast, then the other, with his mouth, she slid her hands up inside his sweater so that she could grip his warm flesh with an urgency of her own. It was the first time she had explored a man's body so intimately, and she marvelled at the lean hardness of it, fingering each separate rib under her hands until she reached the inward curve of his waist. Her progress was impeded by his trouser belt and she gave it a little impatient tug.

Only when he reached to help her with the buckle, did she come to her senses. This was madness. She had not only let him touch her in a way no man ever had before, but she was as eager for his caresses as any of the girls she had called wanton at the Academy.

'No, please,' she protested, meaning it this time.

'You know you want me and I want you, isn't that enough?' he coaxed.

She struggled free and retreated to her corner of the seat, cowering there. 'I'm not a tease, honestly. I just lost my head for a minute.'

'I guess we both did,' he said grimly. 'Don't look so frightened. I'm not going to take you against your will.'

She breathed a great shuddering sigh of relief. 'I don't know what came over me.'

'Well, I do. Honest human passion, perhaps for the first time in your life. I warned you that you had it in you.'

With that, he got out of the car and slammed the door behind him. In the blackness, she saw the flare of a cigarette lighter, then the red glow of his cigarette as he drew on it. Damn him! Why did he have to be right? She had succumbed to passion in a way she hadn't known she was capable of doing.

Desperately, she began to catalogue the things she disliked about him—his money and his arrogant use of the power it gave him; his age—he was her best friend's father, for pity's sake! What had happened between them couldn't be anything other than physical attraction—it couldn't.

So why did she have this bereft sensation, as if she was a piece of human flotsam which had been washed up on the beach of his personality?

CHAPTER SIX

How could she have behaved so wantonly? she asked herself over and over again. She had hoped that a little time would be all she needed to recover her composure, but a week after the scene with Russell in the car, she still felt as confused as ever.

The painting she was supposed to be working on sat half-finished and neglected in front of her as she tried yet again to come to terms with what had happened.

'Honest human passion,' Russell had called it. But was it honest to betray her own convictions in the heat of a moment? He was everything she disliked in a man, and yet she had allowed him to take liberties with her which she had denied to any other man.

So what did that make her?

She shuddered to think of an answer, because it was becoming painfully obvious. Russell had called her a sexy lady, making it sound like a desirable quality, but it was really a polite way of saying she was so weak she didn't possess the willpower to say no.

It was different for him. To him, she was probably just one of many conquests. Wasn't he known as a ladies' man around the district? Someone as wealthy and eligible as he was could no doubt have his pick of the women on the Peninsula. She almost laughed aloud. Of them both, she was probably the only one giving the incident a moment's thought.

He hadn't seemed worried about it during the rest of the interminable wait for Robin to arrive, she recalled. He had been angry with her, but that was probably because he had been denied his own way. She had the feeling he didn't like being denied anything he really wanted.

'Serve him right,' she said aloud. It would do him good to realise that his money wasn't enough to buy everything he wanted.

She had watched nervously as he paced up and down outside the car, smoking one cigarette after another in the blackness. After a while, she started to worry that he might catch a chill and had wound down the car window. 'Don't you think you would be warmer in here?'

'I recall it got a little too warm in there for your taste,' he retorted.

Subdued, she closed the window again and sank back against the upholstery. Now he was blaming her for the whole thing. It wasn't fair. Tears squeezed their way out from under her tightly closed lids and she dashed them away angrily. How she hated him! If only she had persuaded Barbara not to go into the boutique, none of this would have happened. Barbara would be the one spending the holiday with Russell. As his daughter, she wouldn't have had to cope with his overpowering masculinity as Shandy had been forced to do.

Suddenly, brilliant lights flooded the interior of the car and she had to shield her eyes until they adjusted. It was Robin in the four-wheel-drive, come to look for them as Russell had predicted.

In the light, she became aware of her dishevelled state and made a belated attempt to tidy herself up. One of her buttons must have been loose to begin with, because it had come off when Russell undid her blouse and was nowhere to be found.

She clutched the gaping garment as she got out of the car. Robin's shrewd gaze took in the state of her clothes, but he made no comment. Instead, he said, 'I'll bet you're glad to see me.'

'Regular knight in shining armour,' Russell said sourly.

'Well, don't all rush to thank me at once,' Robin joked, but she saw the puzzlement in his expression. If he had been wondering what he had interrupted, Russell's lack of welcome would have told him more clearly than words. 'She's been giving you trouble, Russell?' he asked, gesturing towards the broken-down car.

Russell chose to interpret the remark his own way and looked straight at Shandy, his expression accusing. 'You've got no idea.'

'What was it? Flat battery?'

'We just couldn't get it going.' Russell said in the same ambiguous tone. Then in a more level voice, he added, 'My guess is the problem's in the starter motor.'

The two men had poked and prodded at the engine by lamplight for a few minutes while she stood by helplessly; then they gave up and announced they would lock the car and leave it where it was for the night. 'We can tow it back in the morning and go to work on it there,' Robin said as he wiped his oily hands on a rag.

That had been a week ago, and since then Russell had been cold and withdrawn towards her. Once or twice she had felt his gaze on her but had avoided meeting his eyes. If he felt cheated by her it was his problem. She hadn't wanted to stay here and she certainly hadn't wanted his attentions.

A small voice inside her argued that she wasn't being entirely honest with herself by saying that. She hadn't resisted when he pressed his lips against hers, nor had she tried to stop him unbuttoning her blouse so that he could have his fill of her pliant flesh. In fact, she had encouraged him with her own touch and returned his kisses with equal ardour.

One thing she was certain of—she couldn't stay at Chedoona Downs any longer. However valid his reasons for keeping her here might be, they were overridden by her urgent need to get away before she succumbed to him completely. The problem was—how? She had tried enlisting Robin's help and failed miserably. Helen Crossley hardly ever went into Ceduna, and she didn't know any of the station hands well enough to risk asking them. But there had to be a way and she was determined to find it, if she had to walk all the way to Ceduna.

'Ah, there you are.'

She looked up as Helen Crossley emerged from the house carrying a laden tray. 'I hope I'm not interrupting your work, but I thought you'd like some morning tea.'

Since the night of the breakdown, Shandy's appetite had deserted her, but she had thought she was concealing it well by playing with her food until the plate was taken away. Now, as Helen stood over her, she knew the housekeeper hadn't been fooled.

To please her, Shandy lifted the embroidered cloth covering the tray. Freshly baked date bread spread with farm butter nestled beside a pot of tea and two cups. 'It looks delicious,' she murmured with what she hoped was enthusiasm.

'And I'm going to stay here until you eat it,' Helen said firmly. 'What you've been eating lately wouldn't keep a mouse alive. I hope you aren't coming down with something.'

'Oh no, nothing like that.' To demonstrate, Shandy took a bite of date bread. It melted in her mouth, making it easy to make a pretence of having an appetite.

She should have known that wouldn't be enough to

satisfy the eagle-eyed housekeeper. Helen settled down beside her in the other canvas chair, and poured two cups of tea. 'I hope you don't mind if I have mine with you.'

There was nothing for it but to sip the tea and eat the rest of the bread. Surprisingly, the food did make her feel a little better. Helen watched the colour seep back into her cheeks and nodded approvingly. 'That's more like it.' She paused for a moment. 'You don't have a mother, do you, Shandy?'

Surprised by the question, Shandy shook her head. 'Both my parents were killed in a boating accident after I left school.'

'So I was told. Will you mind if I offer you some motherly advice?'

Uneasily, Shandy nodded. 'Of course not.'

'Go home to Adelaide and get yourself some young friends you can have fun with.' Catching Shandy's startled reaction, she continued hastily, 'It isn't that I don't enjoy having you here, far from it. As I said when you arrived, it's a pleasant change to have some female company. But you're not doing yourself any good moping around here, making yourself miserable over something you can't have.'

Shandy almost choked on her cup of tea. So Robin had been right, his mother did see herself as the next Mrs Stratton and was warning Shandy away. 'I see,' she said slowly.

'I'm glad you do,' Helen said, satisfied. 'I know you young people don't take kindly to advice of any kind, but I felt I had to say something. You're not enjoying yourself here, anyone can see that. I'm surprised that the Boss hasn't said anything about it himself.'

Shandy knew why Russell hadn't commented about her withdrawn state. He had been so vexed with her over the incident in the car that he had been avoiding her ever since. When they did speak, he seemed to be controlling his temper with an effort, so he was not likely to waste any time worrying over her.

'I suppose he's been too busy,' she said flatly.

'Getting ready for the harvest is always a busy time around here. It eases off once the wheat is in, until autumn when they start burning off and ploughing.' She laughed lightly. 'You should be flattered that Russell's given up as much time for you as he has. I've never known him to do that for anyone, not even Della.'

Was this Helen's way of telling her that she had taken up enough of Russell's time and should now bow out gracefully? If only she could, she thought wildly.

Helen replaced her cup on the tray and stood up. 'I'd better leave you to your work.'

Shandy drained her cup and added it to the tray. 'Thanks for the refreshments,' she said. And for the motherly advice, she added to herself.

'My pleasure,' Helen assured her and carried the tea things back inside.

Watching her go, Shandy had trouble believing that such a pleasant woman could have a devious nature. It didn't seem possible from what she had come to know of Helen Crossley. But what was the saying about a woman scorned? Maybe she was likeable only as long as her future wasn't threatened.

Not that Shandy meant to threaten it. Whatever Helen imagined, there was nothing between her and Russell Stratton. The scene in the car had been a moment of sexual weakness, nothing more. Helen was not to know that if there was any way she could get away from Chedoona Downs, she would take it without a backward glance.

In a fit of temper, she attacked the painting with renewed vigour, completing it swiftly with bold, slashing brush strokes that were quite unlike her usual restrained style.

'Oh! That's very good.'

She had been working so intently that she hadn't heard a car drive up until her reverie was disturbed by the arrival of Russell's cousin Anna and her husband, George, both of whom Shandy remembered meeting on her visit to Thevenard.

She smiled warmly, liking Anna. 'I'm glad you like my work. I was . . . experimenting with a new style.'

'It's the Bight, isn't it? Don't tell me—Davenport Creek.'

'Right first time,' came another voice, and Shandy tensed as Russell strode up to them. 'I took Shandy swimming there when we did the round trip to Penong.'

He studied the painting critically. 'Yes, it is good, but much more aggressive than your usual style, Shandy. Why the change?'

She couldn't very well tell him that she had channelled into the painting all her pent-up fury against him. Luckily, the scene was a seascape, so the slashing brush strokes suited the turbulent surf along the Nullarbor Cliffs. If it had been the type of pastoral scene she usually liked to paint, she would have had more trouble explaining the resentment the brush-strokes revealed.

'Shandy told me she was experimenting,' Anna supplied for her.

His eyes bored into her like twin gimlets and she had the uncomfortable feeling that he could see all the way to her soul. 'She's done quite a bit of experimenting since she came here, haven't you, Shandy?

She decided to ignore the double meaning. 'I'll probably go back to my old ways when I leave here,' she said airily.

'Hasn't anyone told you—life doesn't allow you to go back,' he said grimly.

He was right about that. She would never be able to return to her old ways of thinking, he had seen to that. The virtuous image of herself that she had nurtured was shattered forever. But he would never shake her conviction that too much money was an affliction rather than a blessing. If anything, he had strengthened her belief by the arrogant way he used the power his money gave him.

'You are staying for lunch?' Russell asked Anna, taking her assent for granted. 'Of course, Shandy will be joining us.'

Since the painting was obviously finished she had no good excuse to avoid lunching with them. It would be one of the few meals she and Russell had shared since that fateful night. On most other occasions, one or the other of them had found some excuse not to come to the table.

With Anna and George sharing the meal, it wasn't as bad as Shandy had feared. She pretended great interest in the fishing industry at Thevenard so that she could spend most of the time talking to George.

Although he looked darkly Greek, George's accent was purely Australian. As well as owning several of the fishing boats based at Thevenard, he was director of one of the fish processing plants.

'I'd like to see it if I may,' Shandy said as an idea occurred to her. If she could persuade George to take her to visit the plant she might have a chance to slip away to the airport afterwards.

'You don't mean that, surely?' Anna said, wrinkling her nose delicately. 'Have you any idea what a fish processing plant smells like?'

'Fish, I suppose,' Shandy supplied and wondered why everyone laughed at her.

'Like the worst fish smell you can possibly imagine,' George explained. 'Not the sort of place anyone would visit for entertainment.'

Shandy could see her opportunity slipping away, but she could think of no way to persuade George without arousing Russell's suspicions.

He was aware of her strategy, however, because he smiled disarmingly at her. 'As an artist, Shandy feels that she should do all and see all, even the unpleasant things. Am I right?'

'Er . . . yes,' she replied, not sure what he was driving at.

'In that case, why don't I show you the processing plant? There's no need to trouble George, since I have to go to Ceduna tomorrow in any case. I can show you around, then we can have lunch in town afterwards.'

There was no way she was going to spend another day in his company. 'Since nobody else seems to think it's a good idea, I think I'll stay here and paint tomorrow,' she demurred.

'If you're sure?' he said with a mocking glint in his dark eyes.

'Quite sure.' She wished he would drop the whole question. To her relief, he obliged, and the conversation moved on to other matters. She let the talk eddy and flow around her. So he was going to Ceduna tomorrow, was he? Well, she was going with him—but he wouldn't know it, because she intended to stow away. It would take careful planning and good timing, but she could do it. When he parked the car in Ceduna, she would let herself out and be gone before he knew she had even left the property.

'What's so amusing?' George asked, breaking into her thoughts.

She realised she had allowed her glee to show on her face, and quickly schooled her features into a semblance of calmness. 'Oh, I was just thinking of a joke I heard.'

'Like to share it with us, Shandy?' Russell asked with a steely edge to his voice.

'I'm no good at telling jokes, really,' she said.

The tension between them grew palpable, and she saw Anna's puzzled gaze flicker from her to Russell. Anna gave George a gentle nudge. 'Weren't you going to take a look at Russell's new air seeder?' she said pointedly.

'What? Oh yes, I was. Like to give me a guided tour, Russ?'

His expression still grim, Russell pushed his chair away from the table and led the way outside. Their voices became a distant murmur as they headed in the direction of the machinery shed.

Anna play-acted wiping her brow. 'Whew! What's got into Russ to make him so difficult? I've never seen him so touchy before except when . . . just before Della left.'

'It's my fault, I suppose,' Shandy confessed miserably.

Anna looked at her keenly. 'Your fault? In what way?'

'I . . . I wasn't supposed to be here. His daughter was the one who was meant to come. The plans got a bit mixed up and he . . . he got stuck with me instead.'

'You don't strike me as being hard to get along with. But if you and Russ don't get along, why do you stay?'

'He thought it was a good idea at first. Now, I think he's regretting it.' All that was true enough as far as it went. There was no reason to involve Anna in the real circumstances of her arrival at Chedoona Downs.

'I see,' Anna said softly, although it was plain from her expression that she didn't really. Then a glimmer of understanding lit up her attractive face. 'Oh-oh. Have you gone and fallen in love with Russ?'

'No, of course not,' Shandy denied a shade too quickly. 'That is . . . I don't know. I just know he makes me madder than any man ever did before.'

Anna nodded. 'Sounds like love to me.' Impulsively, she covered Shandy's hand with hers. 'Imagine falling for a tough nut like Russell. After what Della did to him, I'd be surprised if he ever trusted a woman again.'

Shandy turned imploring eyes on the other woman. 'What did Della do? I've heard something about her being bored with country life, but I've a feeling that isn't the whole story. And I think I have the right to know.'

'You have a right to know why Russell's the way he is, I suppose. Mostly it was her fault.' Anna took a deep breath. 'When you came to Thevenard, you said you were a friend of Barbara's. Do you know when her birthday is?'

Shandy was puzzled. 'Yes. December fifth. But what . . .'

Anna held up a quieting hand. 'Della and Russell were married in late June. Barbara was born the same year.'

For a moment, the point Anna was making eluded Shandy; then her eyes widened. 'But that means . . .'

'Exactly. You can count. So, alas, could Russell. The child wasn't his.'

'How could he be so sure?'

Anna smiled gently. 'There is a thing among Greeks. We call it *filotimo*—a born-in sense of personal honour, of pride. Russell swore on that honour that he had not slept with Della before they were married. No-one who knows him would doubt such an oath.'

Involuntarily, Shandy drew in her breath, then let it out again slowly. 'Poor Russell.'

The sadness in Anna's eyes echoed Shandy's reaction. 'Yes, poor Russell. But even though he had been tricked into marriage to provide a father for her child, he vowed to stand by Della and raise the child as his own. He made Barbara his heir and came to love her as if she was his flesh and blood. He forbade the family to mention the matter ever again.'

With an unsteady hand, Shandy poured more coffee into both cups. 'I still don't understand. If it was all resolved, what went wrong?'

'After Russell found out the truth, Della begged him to forgive her. She swore by all that was holy that she would never betray his trust again. One Christmas, she took Barbara away to Adelaide, supposedly on a shopping trip. Russell had to go to the city unexpectedly and thought he would surprise his wife. He was the one surprised. The flat where she was staying belonged to a grazier friend of Russell's. When he found them together, they admitted they had been meeting secretly for over a year. Della never came back here. Eventually, she and Russell were divorced.'

Deep in thought, Shandy sipped her coffee. 'No wonder Russell feels that women are not to be trusted.' Her heart went out to Barbara, who had been the unwitting pawn in Della's game. What would she say if she knew that it was not her father she should despise, but her mother? Not that Shandy would be the one to tell her. That was up to Della and Russell, not an outsider.

The murmur of voices warned them that the men were returning. Anna touched Shandy's arm. 'Please don't say anything to Russell about this?'

Shandy smiled reassuringly. 'Of course not, but I'm glad you told me.'

'I just wanted you to understand . . .'

'Understand what?' came George's cheerful interjection.

'Women-talk,' Anna said deprecatingly.

As soon as George and Anna left to drive back to Thevenard, Shandy pleaded a headache as an excuse to return to her room. There she stretched out on her bed, her thoughts in turmoil. Was she in love with Russell? She had been so sure that it was only a sexual attraction which would wane as soon as she left Chedoona Downs. After what Anna had told her, there didn't seem to be any chance of anything more developing between them, so what was the point of tormenting herself with thinking about it?

Restlessly, she jumped up and slipped into jeans and a silk shirt, then went outside. Maybe the fresh air would help her to think more clearly.

Outside, she ran into Robin, who was working on the estate car. He straightened up as she approached. 'Hello there. I was beginning to think you weren't speaking to me.'

'Why would you think that?' she asked uncomfortably. 'I've just been busy, that's all. So are you, from the look of things.'

He grimaced at the engine. 'She needed a complete overhaul. I'm still having some problems with the exhaust system, but at least she's operational again. Would you like to start her up for me?'

Glad of something useful to do, Shandy got into the front seat and turned the ignition key. At once, the engine purred into life.

'Okay, that's fine.'

She turned the engine off and walked around to the front of the car. 'Will Russell be taking this car into Ceduna tomorrow?'

Robin nodded. 'She'll need a professional mechanic for the rest of the work. In any case, I'll be using the four-wheel-drive. Is he taking you with him?'

'No, I was just curious.' She held her rising excitement in check and sauntered back to the driver's seat, where she removed the keys and played with them idly. When she was sure Robin wasn't looking, she slid one of the two boot keys off the ring and slipped it into her pocket, then replaced the keys in the ignition. Luckily, she had seen Russell open the boot during the trip to Penong, so she knew which key she needed, and since there was a spare, it was unlikely to be missed.

Although Robin noticed nothing amiss, Shandy's heart was pounding by the time she returned to her room. She told herself that she shouldn't feel guilty, she was being kept here against her will, so it shouldn't surprise Russell if she tried to escape.

At the same time her conscience troubled her. He had been let down so badly by Della; now he was about to be cheated again by Shandy. Why should she care if her action confirmed his view that women were deceitful and traitorous? She only knew that, for some reason, she did care.

This time, she was better prepared for her escape attempt. She knew the car boot was a roomy one, so she could take most of her possessions with her. Once she left Chedoona, she was sure she never wanted to return.

The paintings she had completed since coming here were stacked against a wall, and she gathered them into her portfolio. They were some of her best work, she knew, because she had been so inspired by the beauty and grandeur of the coastline and the arid Nullarbor Plains, as well as the ruggedness of Chedoona itself.

But however beautiful, it was still Heartbreak Plains,

she reminded herself unhappily. The name might have referred to a land which the pioneers were unable to tame, but to her it had a more personal connotation. She had been heart-whole when she arrived, but now—she wasn't so sure.

Whether she was truly in love with Russell or infatuated by his strong sex appeal didn't really matter. After his experience with Della, there was no way he would trust himself to love again, so the best thing she could do was get away from here as soon as possible and try to forget him.

When she went down to dinner, Helen informed her that Russell was lecturing at the Agricultural College as he did regularly, so he wouldn't be joining them. Shandy tried to mask her relief. She had been afraid that he would sense she was plotting something and find a way to thwart her.

So that neither Robin nor Helen would notice anything amiss, she made an effort to be outgoing during dinner and even managed to eat a generous helping of Helen's steak and kidney pie and garden-fresh vegetables.

'I'm glad to see you've got your appetite back,' Helen commented, smiling knowingly at her. 'I hope my little talk this morning did some good.'

'What little talk?' Robin asked, helping himself to more pie.

'Oh, just gossiping,' Helen said dismissively. 'By the way, how's Linda?'

'She's on night shift at the moment, which is why we haven't seen much of her. But she goes back on to days next week, so she'll be up to visit us then.'

Linda was Robin's fiancée, Shandy gathered. She recalled Russell saying he was engaged to a nurse at the Ceduna hospital. Fleetingly, she wondered why Helen was going to such trouble to bring her into the conversation now, after hardly mentioning her all week. Maybe Helen was worried that, having been warned off Russell, Shandy might turn to Robin, so she was making it clear that he was 'spoken for'.

Heavens! Why did they all think of her as such a man-chaser? First there was Helen's little chat this morning, then Anna's more gentle but unequivocal warning that Russell had no time for women. Even Russell himself had gone to great lengths to ensure that she didn't become involved with Robin.

She sighed deeply. If only she could explain that she wasn't interested in Russell *or* Robin! However attracted she might be to Russell, there were too many barriers between them which prevented any sort of relationship from growing, even supposing she wanted it to. As for Robin, he was likeable, but she couldn't see herself getting romantically involved with him. She realised that, unconsciously, she had been comparing him with Russell, a habit she would have to get out of or she would spend the rest of her life trying to find someone who embodied Russell's disturbing masculinity, dark good looks and powerful personality.

Still, it was difficult to avoid making comparisons. The warmth of his touch had seared her skin like a brand, and his lips had marked hers so indelibly that she would forever compare any other embrace to his.

'I hope he's good-looking,' Robin teased.

'What?' She came back to awareness of her surroundings as a rush of colour flooded her cheeks, betraying the accuracy of his taunt.

'It was a man!' he laughed. 'You're actually blushing.'

'Leave the girl alone,' Helen said firmly. 'Don't take any notice of him, Shandy. It's a pleasure to see a girl innocent enough that she can still blush. There aren't too many these days.'

Since she had never thought of the tiresome habit as a virtue, Shandy lowered her eyes. Did Russell find her blushes becoming? she couldn't help wondering. Probably the opposite since they emphasised the chasm between his experience and her innocence.

She was relieved when she was finally able to escape to her room. As she retrieved her luggage from its hiding place under the bed, she had an uncomfortable sense of déjà vu. This time, however, no-one else knew of her plans, so Russell couldn't outwit her again.

She waited until she heard the front door close as Helen and Robin returned to their own quarters; then she allowed another half-hour to elapse for good measure before creeping down the stairs and out into the courtyard. The estate car was parked undercover, but the shed was unlocked and she stole quietly into it.

Using the borrowed key,, she opened the boot and stowed her luggage away, leaving the centre space empty for herself. She debated whether to get into the space now, but decided against it. The trip into town would be uncomfortable enough in such cramped quarters. There was no point in making the ordeal any longer than it had to be.

Although she tried not to fall asleep, the morning cock-crow roused her from a deep slumber, and for a moment she couldn't recall why she was curled in an armchair, fully dressed. Then she remembered. Good lord, the time! If Russell planned to leave as early as before, she would have to hurry to reach the car before he did.

His late night lecturing must have had an effect, because the car was deserted when she got there and climbed into the boot. A few minutes later she heard his firm tread. The car rocked as he got in, then the engine came to life and they moved off.

The ride was much more uncomfortable than she'd anticipated, and it was so hot that perspiration poured from her. If only she hadn't overslept, she could have at least had something cool to drink before getting into the car. At the very thought of liquid, her throat constricted in protest. Dust from inside the boot teased at her nose and throat, making her feel even drier. She couldn't remember when she had been so thirsty.

A sob of despair escaped from her throat. If she felt so badly now, what state would she be in by the time they reached Ceduna? She tried to tell herself it wasn't far, but the corrugated dirt roads made every mile seem like two.

Abruptly, the car stopped and she heard voices nearby. ''Morning, Boss.' She recognised the voice of one of the jackeroos.

''Morning, Mitch,' Russell responded. 'Everything geared up for the harvest?'

'Oh, please don't make it a long conversation,' she implored silently. The air in the boot was already stale and she started to feel light-headed. She tugged at the collar of her shirt to try to ease her breathing.

The men chatted for several minutes and she almost cried with relief when she heard Russell say, 'Righto! I'll be out to give you a hand when I've been to town.'

Once more, they began to move, but no hint of a breeze reached her hiding place. She had stopped perspiring and wondered if that was a sign of dehydration. She giggled helplessly. Imagine if Russell didn't open the boot for ages. All he'd find would be her bleached bones among her possessions. Would he be sorry?

'Who's sorry now?' she began to croon to herself. Oh

dear! She felt very peculiar. What was that funny smell in the air? She was sure she hadn't noticed it before.

Distantly, alarm bells began to ring in her head. There was something she ought to remember—but what? Petrol? No, she would recognise that. Her head ached as she tried to marshal her thoughts. Robin had said there was something wrong with the exhaust system. Carbon monoxide—could that be the smell? Oh God, if it was and she didn't get out of here soon, she would be poisoned!

Frantically, she fumbled with the boot latch, but something had happened to her fingers, making them stiff and awkward. In desperation, she hammered on the inside of the boot lid. 'Russell! Russell, help me!' Maybe he couldn't hear her over the drone of the engine.

Then, miraculously, the car screeched to a halt and she heard his footsteps hurrying around to the back of the car.

Light flooded into her hiding place and she threw her hands up in front of her face to shield her eyes. 'Russell?' she whimpered.

'My God—Shandy!' Sweet relief coursed through her as she felt herself being lifted gently out and placed on the back seat of the car, then inky blackness closed over her.

Moments later, she opened her eyes to find him staring down at her with cold fury. 'What the devil were you doing in there?'

'I . . . I wanted to get away,' she croaked through parched lips. Her head was splitting. 'I'm so thirsty.'

With a muffled oath, he fetched the canvas waterbag which always swung from the front bumper bar, and held the bag while she drank from it. The mineral-laden water tasted like champagne! 'That's better,' she gasped, wiping the droplets from her chin and mouth. Russell was watching her through blazing eyes, and she became alarmed at his stillness. 'Don't be angry,' she implored.

'Angry! For two pins I'd turn you over my knee and beat some sense into you. Don't you realise you could have died in there?'

The terror she'd felt when she thought she might suffocate returned, and she began to tremble. 'It was stupid, I can see that now. But it was the only way I could think of to get to Ceduna.'

He tightened his grip on the waterbag and his knuckles whitened. 'You hate me so much that you'd risk your life to get away from me?'

'No! It's not that, it's just . . .' she tailed off in despair. How could she explain that it was for precisely the opposite reason that she had to get away?

'No need to spell it out, I get the picture,' he said harshly. 'I'll take you to Ceduna airport if it's so important for you.'

She nodded miserably. She was still weak and her head ached from her ordeal, but she felt much better now she had slaked her thirst and could breathe fresh air. All she wanted was to get away from here and lick her emotional wounds.

'Are you well enough to travel?' he asked, his tone flat and emotionless.

'Yes, thanks.'

'Then tidy yourself up and we'll drive straight to the airport.'

The drive was completed in silence. On the way, she restored order to her hair and clothes. At the airport, Russell asked her to wait in the car while he arranged her flight. He was back in minutes.

'You're lucky. There's a flight in half an hour,' he said, handing her a ticket and her luggage.

She couldn't just leave like this. 'Russell, I . . .'

'Have a safe flight,' he said in the same flat tone. Tears

began to prickle the backs of her eyes, and she turned away, but he caught at her arm. 'I'm really sorry things turned out the way they did.'

'Yes,' she agreed huskily, 'so am I.'

On impulse, he reached into his wallet and took out a white card. 'I have an office and an apartment in Adelaide. The address is on here. If you ever need anything . . .'

'Thanks.' She accepted the card and dropped it into her handbag, but as she walked away, she was sure she would never have cause to use it.

CHAPTER SEVEN

'MORE coffee, Sarah?'

'Mmm, please.' Shandy's neighbour looked appreciatively around the small flat. 'I really must do something with my flat. Every time I come into yours, I feel ashamed to go home to mine.'

'Most of this is the landlord's doing,' Shandy admitted. 'All the furniture, the drapes, carpets and so on came with the place.'

She and Barbara had been lucky to get this flat, she knew. It had only been possible because the landlord was a friend of Della's, otherwise there was no way he would have let it to two student models. The apartment had been professionally decorated before they moved in, and Shandy found the bisque walls and apricot carpeting soothing to return home to. She particularly loved the spreading gum tree outside her bedroom window, and the view across the Glenelg beach from the other windows.

Although the apartment wasn't large, what space there was had been used to good advantage. The kitchen was an extension of the living room, separated from it by see-through shelves acting as a room divider. The living room led on to two side-by-side bedrooms, one for each of them, both with large windows looking out on to the gum tree. Shandy's room also boasted a view of the ocean from one side.

In each bedroom, floor-to-ceiling sliding doors on tracks took up one whole wall, concealing a huge amount of wardrobe space. Characteristically, in Barbara's feminine pink bedroom, every inch of the wardrobe was crammed with designer clothes and dozens of pairs of shoes.

By contrast, Shandy's room was simply furnished with a divan bed covered in hand-loomed Indian fabric, a small table and cane storage chest. Her wardrobe was mainly used to house her painting things, with her small collection of clothes relegated to the last third.

Shandy jumped when Sarah snapped two fingers under her nose. 'What was that for?'

'You were miles away. I thought this holiday was supposed to fortify you, not wear you out.'

'It hasn't worn me out.'

Sarah laughed. 'Oh no? Ever since you came home you've been wandering around in a daze. Twice I've said good morning to you on the stairs, and been totally ignored.'

'Oh, I'm sorry,' Shandy replied, 'I didn't mean to do that.'

'No harm done.' Sarah leaned forward conspiratorially. 'You're in love, aren't you? I'll bet it's that gorgeous Jordan Cole, your blissfully single-and-not-gay-for-once mentor.'

'No, I'm not in love—and most certainly not with Jordan Cole,' Shandy said firmly. She hadn't told anyone that her holiday had been spent on the Eyre Peninsula instead of at the artists' colony in the Flinders Ranges, so naturally Sarah thought she had been with Jordan. 'He and I are . . .'

'. . . just good friends, I know,' Sarah finished for her. 'Okay, I know when to mind my own business.' She drained her coffee cup and stood up. 'I'd better be going or my own mentor will be wondering where his dinner is. When's Barbara due back?'

'Any day now. I've forgotten the exact date, if she ever got around to telling me.'

'That sounds like Barbara. Lucky thing, going off to Noumea for three weeks!'

'Yes, lucky Barbara,' Shandy agreed a little sourly. But for a twist of fate, Barbara would have been the one spending the last weeks at Chedoona Downs, instead of Shandy. How different everything would have been then!

She closed the front door behind Sarah and absently started clearing away the coffee things. Sarah was right. She had been walking around in a daze since coming home from Ceduna. Sometimes, she wondered if a part of her had been left behind on the Peninsula.

Could Sarah have been right about that, too? Was it her heart that had been left behind?

'No!' she said aloud. She couldn't possibly be in love with Russell Stratton on the strength of three weeks' acquaintance. Yet she knew couples who had fallen in love and become happily married on the strength of three *minutes* in each other's company. Except that in their case, there had been no conflict of beliefs and lifestyle to get in the way of their happiness. Far too many barriers existed between herself and Russell. He was too much older and more experienced to be satisfied with her youthful innocence. And, she had to face it, he enjoyed manipulating people, using the power his wealth provided. That was the hardest thing to accept. She knew through bitter experience that money could never buy happiness. In the case of her parents, it had destroyed them.

Even if she could come to terms with all that, Russell would never trust a woman again. He might take her to bed—she shivered at the prospect, remembering how thoroughly he had aroused her that night in his car—but he would never allow her into his heart.

Disconsolately, she wandered into her bedroom. Around the walls were ranged the paintings she had done at Ceduna, and her heart ached as she looked at them. There was the old crab fisherman dangling his wicker pots off the town jetty; the surf pounding aggressively against the Nullarbor Cliffs; a scene of arid desolation on the Nullarbor itself with a string of camels visible on the far horizon; and the sketches she had made at Chedoona itself. Surrounded by them, she felt momentarily as if she was back there, feeling the hot outback sun on her shoulders and seeing again the golden fields of ripening wheat. Mechanically, she gathered the pictures up and slid them into her zippered portfolio which she stowed in her wardrobe.

Damn Russell! If she wasn't in love with him, why did he and his country haunt her so?

Her easel was set up in a corner of her room and the pristine cartridge paper beckoned to her. At once, she knew what she would do—if she couldn't get Russell out of her system any other way, why not paint him out!

Never before had she worked with such confidence or intensity. The brush became an extension of her hand and the colours flowed across the paper with unerring ease. It was as if the painting already existed on the paper, needing only her hand to uncover the details and reveal it to the world.

Occasionally, she glanced out of the window, seeking inspiration from the ocean that rolled onto Glenelg beach a block away. She didn't see the beach or the sightseers—she was hundreds of miles away in mid-Pacific, aboard a many-masted schooner, capturing the likeness of her captain with her brush.

When the daylight faded, she paused long enough to switch on a light, then returned to work with feverish preoccupation. She hardly noticed when night merged imperceptibly with the dawn of a new day.

Finally, she cast down her brush with a satisfied sigh. 'There, you arrogant pirate—captured, and by a woman, yet. What do you think of that?'

As she stepped back, her subject seemed to loom over her from the easel. She had painted him astride the deck of his schooner, with one hand clasped around a spar. His black, black hair was ruffled by a sea breeze, and the dark eyes seemed almost as black as the hair, except for the spark of roguish amusement she had added. A flowing white shirt, split to the waist, revealed a tanned torso rippling with muscles, and the loose sleeves caught at each wrist masked, without completely concealing, the powerful shoulders and upper arms. Her gaze travelled down his body, noting with satisfaction how she had rendered the muscular shape of his thighs so that they seemed to be seeking escape from the tight knee-breeches.

Yes, she could imagine such a man boarding a British brig and gallantly reassuring her crew, while he made off with everything of value. Rogue, pirate . . . lover.

'Yes, lover,' the sardonic twist of his mouth seemed to say. In that split second she realised she had not captured him at all. He had captured her.

For the pirate she had painted was Russell Stratton, and she was finally forced to accept that she had fallen in love with him. She had painted him as his errant ancestor, but the features were unmistakable, because she had poured into the picture all the love she had been denying to herself.

Despairingly, she covered her face with her hands. 'Oh God!' Even if she could overcome her fear of everything he represented, he had no room in his heart for any woman. What was she going to do?

Like a robot, she began to clear away the painting things, feeling the exhaustion of her all-night marathon catching up with her rapidly. Now that her obsession had spent itself, she felt drained and empty.

'Anybody home?'

The scraping of a key in the lock brought her to her senses. Barbara! She mustn't see the painting of her father, at all costs. She knew Shandy far too well to misinterpret the message in the picture. Frantically, she scanned the room for a suitable hiding place. Barbara's footsteps came closer, so she thrust the still-wet painting under her bed, then straightened quickly as her flatmate came in.

'There you are! When you didn't answer, I thought you must be out.'

'No. I . . . I was working and lost track of the time.'

Barbara took in Shandy's dishevelled appearance and blood-streaked eyes, then looked at the empty easel. 'Are you all right?' she asked worriedly.

'Yes, I'm fine. Give me a minute, then I'll join you for a cup of tea and hear all about the trip.'

'All right. I'll just put my gear in my room,' Barbara agreed, her tone still doubtful. 'You're sure everything's all right?'

'Yes, I said so,' Shandy snapped, then checked her temper with an effort. 'I'm sorry, Barbie, you caught me in a bad moment, that's all. I . . . I've got a headache.'

Slightly mollified, Barbara left her alone, promising to return with some aspirin after she had settled in. Soon she could be heard bustling around her own room, and Shandy relaxed slightly. She looked around the room. The painting was probably as safe under the bed as anywhere, so she decided to leave it there. When it was dry, she could store it among the rest of her work. Then she folded the easel, finished clearing away the rest of her things and packed everything into the wardrobe.

Now she had finally admitted her true feelings, she longed for some time alone to study them and marvel at their novelty. But that would have to wait until later. Barbara was probably bursting with news about the trip and would be hurt if Shandy insisted on being left alone.

Resignedly, she went out to the bathroom and washed the paint off her hands, then splashed cool water over her face and eyes which were puffy with tiredness. The cold water felt blissful, so she soaked some cotton wool and stood with the pads pressed against her burning eyes.

'These are for you,' Barbara said behind her.

She removed the pads to find her flatmate holding out a glass of water and two tablets. Remembering that she was supposed to have a headache, she smiled gratefully and took them. As soon as Barbara went back to the kitchen, she poured the tablets and water down the sink.

'Feeling better now?' Barbara asked when Shandy joined her in the kitchen.

'Yes, thanks.' She accepted a cup of tea and sipped it, glad to have something to do with her hands. Carefully, she set the cup down and forced herself to look cheerful. 'You're looking very well, I must say. What a super tan.'

'Haven't I?' Barbara agreed, distracted as Shandy had hoped she would be. 'There was little else to do but lie in the sun or swim. Our hotel had about ten staff for every guest. And Armand taught me to wind-surf.'

Shandy raised an eyebrow questioningly. 'Armand?'

Suddenly shy, Barbara lowered her eyes. 'He was the assistant manager of the hotel. He wasn't really supposed to mix with the guests socially, but he found an excuse to dance with me every night. Oh Shandy, I think I'm in love.'

At another time, Shandy would have advised Barbara against reading too much into a holiday romance. But what was her obsession with Russell if not the same thing? She was in no position to offer advice. When no censure was forthcoming, Barbara went on breathlessly: 'He's so tall and sophisticated. I was the envy of every girl there.' She jumped to her feet. 'I almost forgot. I brought you some presents.'

She dashed into her room and came out with a parcel bearing the name of an island boutique. Curiously, Shandy undid the wrapping and took out a length of softly draping cloth in shimmering tropical colours. She held it up. 'What lovely fabric!'

Barbara laughed. 'It's a pareo, silly. You wear it in all sorts of ways, like this.' She took the cloth from Shandy and began draping it around her body, first to make an off-the-shoulder dress, then a wraparound skirt, and finally loose pants tied at the waist, and a beach wrap. 'There, see? Everyone wears them in the islands.'

'I can see I'll be a hit on Glenelg beach,' Shandy agreed. Privately she wondered if she would have the courage to wear anything so revealing, but she didn't hurt Barbara's feelings by saying so. She was more genuinely enthusiastic about a coral necklace Barbara gave her, announcing, 'I've bought a similar one for Mother.'

The apricot colour of the coral was truly lovely and complemented the tan Shandy had acquired at Ceduna. Her obvious pleasure pleased Barbara. 'I'm glad you're really feeling better. You should have come with me instead of working the whole time. You'd have gotten a kick out of the casino.'

'You were gambling?' Shandy asked, surprised. 'Did they know how old you are?'

Barbara shrugged. 'I looked as grown-up as anyone there, especially on Armand's arm. I didn't have much luck, though.'

'How much did you lose?'

Barbara named a sum that made Shandy wince. Then she grinned. 'Don't worry about the money—remember, I'm an heiress.'

At once, Shandy's heart went out to the younger girl who was heir to much more than she knew. What would her reaction be if she knew it was her mother who had been the villain in her young life, and not her father as she had been brought up to think? Shandy was very fond of Barbara and wished with all her heart that she could help bring about a reconciliation between Russell and his daughter, but reminded herself that it wasn't her place to interfere.

She let Barbara ramble on about the places she had visited and things she had done on her holiday, but heard only half of what she said. Finally, Barbara stopped to catch her breath. 'That's enough about me. How was the Flinders Ranges?'

'It was very nice,' Shandy said non-committally.

'Nice? You call three weeks of free love with Jordan Cole *nice*?'

'Orana is nothing like that,' she protested. 'And there is nothing between me and Jordan except a common love of art.'

Barbara pouted. 'There's no need to make such a big thing of it.'

'I'm sorry. It's just that you're the second matchmaker I've had in here recently. Sarah was doing the same thing only yesterday.'

'Only because we care about you, Shandy.'

A lump rose to Shandy's throat. 'I know, and the feeling's mutual.'

Brightening at once, Barbara grinned. 'How about showing me the work you did in the Ranges?'

This was a moment Shandy had been dreading. She couldn't show any of her paintings to Barbara without giving away where she had been, and telling the truth would further alienate Barbara from her father. 'You're not interested in a lot of gum trees,' she said. 'Besides, I haven't finished any of them properly.'

Barbara was about to protest when the doorbell pealed. As one, both girls put down their cups and chorused, 'I'll get it.' They looked at one another and laughed.

'I'll go,' supplied Barbara. 'It's probably Mother anyway. I rang her from the airport and she said she'd drop in later.'

Not much later, Shandy noticed cynically. She had never really liked Barbara's mother, and since she had learned how Della had treated Russell, she had even less cause to do so. She had to make an effort to smile as the woman came in. 'Hello, Della.'

'Good morning, Shandy.' They touched cheeks and Shandy was enveloped in a cloud of spicy French perfume. Then Della hugged Barbara and perched herself elegantly on a bar stool. Shandy was reminded of Monica Giles at the academy, admonishing the students that 'a lady only ever has one leg'. As she watched Della tuck one leg neatly against the other, she thought someone must have given her the same advice sometime.

Della could well have been a model, Shandy observed. She had glossy blonde hair, finely chiselled features and skin smooth as alabaster. No wonder she hadn't enjoyed the harsh conditions of the Nullarbor. The sun would have been torture to someone of her skin and colouring. As Della and Barbara chatted about the trip, Shandy tried to picture Della standing on a clifftop on the edge of the Nullarbor Plains. She would probably have been more concerned about the wind disturbing her hairstyle, than the grandeur of the place, she decided. Barbara's use of her own name brought her out of her reverie.

'Shandy disapproves of me gambling, don't you?'

Della was unworried that her daughter had spent part of her holiday in a casino. 'As an heiress, Barbara has to get used to that sort of lifestyle,' she said breezily.

Shandy wondered what Russell would think if he could hear his generosity being taken for granted like this. In the circumstances, he wasn't obliged to make Barbara his heir, as Della, of all people, must appreciate. She wondered how she could ever have been intimidated by Della. Now, she only felt sorry for her. The affair with the grazier couldn't have lasted for long, since he was nowhere in sight now. And though Della had plenty of willing escorts to the many social functions she attended, there was no-one special in her life. What a price she had paid for her folly!

She realised that Della had been speaking to her. 'I'm sorry?'

'I asked whether you would contribute some of your work to a charity art show I'm organising. The charity takes a commission, of course, but the rest goes to the artist.'

Shandy shook her head. 'I'm afraid I don't have anything suitable right now.'

Della frowned. 'I find that hard to believe when you've just spent a vacation in the hills painting gum trees. You must have *something* to show for it.'

'Shandy's behaving very strangely today,' Barbara

contributed. 'She won't even show me what she did while she was away.'

'It isn't like you to be secretive,' Della commented.

If they only knew it, she was doing a lot of things she wouldn't have dreamed of doing before. Her visit to Chedoona Downs seemed to have turned her values upside down. She felt completely changed in some way. 'I'm sorry, the pictures aren't ready for showing,' she said firmly. Although plainly displeased, Della had no choice but to accept this.

The remaining days of their vacation sped by. Della took Barbara shopping for new clothes for the coming term and offered to take Shandy as well, but since her budget didn't stretch to new outfits, she declined. The clothes she had would have to suffice until she was earning. If she was given any paying assignments during term, as senior students sometimes were, she might have to invest in suitable clothes, but until then, she could save the money.

'Just think, your last term as a student,' Barbara said enviously. 'After that you'll be a fully-fledged member of the Monica Giles Agency.'

'Provided she decides to keep me on her books,' Shandy supplied.

Barbara laughed. 'As if she'd risk having you snapped up by another agency! Besides, you're already on the headsheets for next summer.'

Shandy stared at her flatmate. The headsheets were posters circulated to advertising agencies and potential clients. They contained photos of all the girls on an agency's books, so that the client could select the type of girl needed for a particular modelling job. 'How did you find that out, assuming it's true?'

Barbara grinned. 'Oh, it's true all right. The proofs

were on Miss Giles' desk when Mother went in to pay my fees last week.'

A great feeling of relief washed over Shandy. She was going to be put on the agency's books after she graduated. Since the Giles Agency was one of the most respected in Adelaide, that meant she could stop worrying about supporting herself. She felt light-headed with relief. Impulsively, she hugged Barbara. 'Better keep that bit of information to yourself or we'll both be thrown out of the Academy,' she cautioned. 'But thanks for telling me.'

'Where are you off to?' Barbara asked when Shandy picked up her bag and headed for the door.

'To celebrate by getting my hair done, what else?'

As she rode the tram downtown, she felt lighter in heart than she had since returning from Chedoona Downs. She still experienced an aching loneliness whenever she allowed herself to think about Russell. But knowing how hopeless it was, she was determined to get on with her life. Barbara's piece of intelligence had given her new hope. With a secure future, she could piece together the remnants of her private life and start again. Surely, in time, she could forget Russell and find someone who would love her as wholly as she was prepared to love in return.

He would probably be a poor, struggling artist, she decided. They would live in a garret, on yoghurt and fresh vegetables, and be blissfully happy. Only occasionally, when she tried to put a face to this artistic paragon, she quickly erased him from her mind, because he insisted on bearing Russell's features.

A professional hairstyle was a rare luxury, and she thoroughly enjoyed being pampered. When she emerged two hours later, she hardly recognised herself. Her straight locks had been coaxed into a new style, shorter at the front and left longer at the back. A hint of curl at the front made her look younger and more carefree. She was glad she had been extravagant for once.

She could hardly wait to get back to the flat to test Barbara's reaction to her new look, but the other girl was nowhere in sight when she walked in. Then she heard sounds coming from the bathroom. Barbara must be experimenting again with her collection of cosmetics, she decided.

While she waited for Barbara to come out, Shandy wandered into her own room and threw her handbag down on the bed. Then she stared in horror at her wardrobe. The sliding door was open and the portfolio of paintings from Ceduna were gone. Anxiously, she searched the rest of the flat, but soon realised that they were not to be found.

She confronted Barbara as soon as she emerged from the bathroom. 'Did you take my paintings?'

Barbara reddened. 'I . . . uh . . . Mother came by and suggested we put them in her art show. She was sure you wouldn't mind.'

'You knew I didn't want them to be shown,' Shandy said despairingly. 'Did you look at them?'

Barbara shook her head. 'I wasn't sure what time you'd be back, so Mother said she would unpack them at the gallery. The show starts tomorrow and they didn't have enough paintings, so it was almost a matter of . . . of life and death.'

If she only knew how close that was to the truth, Shandy agonised. 'Oh, Barbara, how could you?'

Tears clouded Barbara's lovely eyes and her stricken expression touched Shandy. 'I didn't think you'd be so angry,' she whispered. 'I'm sorry, truly.'

'Don't cry, Barbie, it's done now,' Shandy said heavily. She squeezed her flatmate's shoulder reassuringly, then went back into her own room and closed the door. The empty wardrobe mocked her and a sudden cold sensation gripped her. What if . . .

Hastily, she scrabbled underneath the bed and almost wept with relief when her hand closed on a sheet of cartridge paper. Through the paintings, Della couldn't help discovering that Shandy had spent her holiday at Ceduna, but at least her love for Russell was still her secret, locked away in the portrait of him as his pirate ancestor which still lay hidden under the bed. Thank goodness she'd forgotten to put it in the portfolio with the other paintings.

The strident ring of the doorbell interrupted her thoughts and she let out a slow breath. That would be Della, come to demand an explanation. She stood up. Might as well get it over with.

Della was standing in the centre of the living room when Shandy emerged. Her anger was betrayed by two red blotches of colour staining her cheeks, and her hands clenched and unclenched at her sides. Barbara sat curled in an armchair, staring at her mother in bewilderment.

'Hello, Della,' Shandy said evenly.

'Hello, Della,' the other woman mocked. 'Let's dispense with the pleasantries. You know perfectly well why I'm here.'

'I'm afraid I do.'

Unhappily, Barbara looked from one to the other. 'Will somebody please tell me what's going on?'

Della glared at her daughter. 'I found out why Charlotte didn't want us to see any of her precious paintings.'

Barbara's eyes widened. 'Oh? Why not?'

'Because she didn't go to the Flinders Ranges as she led us to believe. Judging from the variety of her work, she spent a good part of the time at Ceduna.'

Puzzled, Barbara stared at Shandy. 'Why didn't you just say you'd gone somewhere different? Surely it wouldn't have made any difference?'

'Not even if she spent the time at Chedoona Downs?'

'Chedoona? With my father?'

Numb with misery, Shandy nodded.

'But why?'

'I'll tell you why,' Della answered for her. 'She's been sneaking around to your father behind our backs, trying to cheat you out of your rightful inheritance. My guess is, it's been her plan all along. It's probably the only reason why she cultivated your friendship in the first place, Barbara.'

This was too much. Shandy jumped to her feet, her eyes blazing. 'That's not true and you've no right to say it.'

Della's fury was a match for Shandy's. 'Oh no? Then why be so underhand about where you went?'

Barbara turned pleading eyes on Shandy. 'Why did you keep it a secret?'

Shandy felt hopelessly trapped. If she told them about the mistaken kidnapping it would only damage the already tenuous relationship between Barbara and her father. However she felt about him, he deserved another chance to get to know his daughter properly. If she told Della what had really happened, no-one connected with Russell would be allowed to come anywhere near Barbara in future. Della might even get a court order to restrain him from seeing her. Even though she wasn't his flesh and blood, it was obvious that he cared so much about Barbara that such an action would shatter him. Shandy couldn't do that to him, so she kept her eyes downcast.

'There, her silence condemns her,' Della said triumphantly.

Barbara was close to tears as she came up to Shandy.

'This afternoon, you asked a question I'd like to ask you back—how could you?'

'What I'd like to know is how long this . . . this sordid affair has been going on?' Della continued relentlessly. 'I've always thought it odd that you should cling to a girl so much younger than yourself—now we know why.'

'It's not true! There's no affair, as you call it. This was the first time . . .'

'. . . the first time you've slept with him?' demanded Della. 'Oh yes, I've got your measure, Charlotte Farrer. I know all about girls like you.'

'Yes, you would, wouldn't you?' Shandy whispered, nearing the limit of her tolerance. Her eyes met Della's and for the first time, she saw real fear in them.

Without taking her eyes off Shandy, she said, 'Barbara, pack your things. You're not staying in this den of iniquity another minute.'

'But Mother . . .'

'Just bring whatever you'll need for tonight,' Della instructed in a tone which forbade any argument. 'We'll send for the rest of your things later.'

Barbara turned towards her room and soon the sounds of doors and drawers opening could be heard, overlaid with muffled sobs. The silence in the living room became oppressive as Della and Shandy remained where they were, facing one another. Shandy felt drained of all emotion. It was even beyond her strength to hate Della for what she was doing. How could she, when she knew Della was reacting out of fear—that Shandy knew the truth about her past and might use it to destroy her?

Nervously, Della began to prowl around the room, picking up ornaments and setting them down again aimlessly. After a few minutes, she whirled towards Shandy. 'How much do you want?'

Caught off-guard, Shandy jumped. 'I don't understand.'

'I presume since you were snooping around Ceduna, you know all about our family skeletons. I want to know how much money it will take to ensure your silence.'

'I don't want money,' Shandy insisted. 'I just . . .'

'You want it all, is that it? His name, his money. So did I, once, and I got it all until I discovered that to a wealthy Greek man—and he is still that, despite his Australian trappings—a wife is a possession, a chattel to be kept at home and shown off on important occasions. You have no life of your own, no rights. I couldn't even see my own friends without his relatives spying on me and reporting back to him.'

If her own friends happened to be male, Shandy could understand Russell's annoyance. But Della could only see her own selfish point of view. She couldn't see that if you loved someone, you didn't betray their trust behind their back. 'You're wrong about everything,' she said quietly. 'Especially in thinking I would stoop to blackmailing you.'

To her surprise, Della laughed harshly. 'I almost wish you would name a price,' she said. 'Then at least I'd know where I stand. I guess I'll just have to wait and see. Because you do have a price, Charlotte—everybody does. But I warn you, Barbara is all I have and I'll fight tooth and nail to protect her. She's had precious little else from Russell, so she's entitled to her inheritance at least.'

'I've told you. I don't want his money,' Shandy said tiredly, her voice becoming hoarse with strain. 'And you needn't worry about Barbara. No matter what I think of you, she's been like a sister to me. I would never do anything to hurt her, and I don't believe Russell would either,' she couldn't help adding.

Della's mouth twisted into a sneer. 'So you're an expert on his thinking too? Not bad for someone who denies having an affair with him. For all the good it will do you.'

She fell silent as Barbara emerged, her face tear-streaked and drawn. She had a suitcase in each hand. Della took one of them from her. 'Let's get out of here.'

At the door, Barbara hesitated and looked back over her shoulder at Shandy, who remained slumped on the sofa. With a little cry, Barbara dropped the case she was carrying and hurled herself at Shandy, hugging her fiercely. 'Shandy, I'm so sorry,' she breathed. Then she picked up her case and followed her mother out of the flat.

As the door slammed shut behind them, Shandy's remaining self-control snapped and she dissolved into a flood of tears, both for herself as the innocent victim in all of this, and for Barbara who didn't know how badly she had been used.

When her sobs finally subsided, she went into the kitchen and shakily made herself a cup of tea. Only then, it occurred to her that she had forgotten to ask Della to return her paintings.

CHAPTER EIGHT

A FEW days later as she rode the tram into Adelaide, Shandy was still wondering why Della had asked her to come over. Probably to return the paintings, she decided, although the other woman had been vague over the phone. Her call had come after a succession of sleepless nights, so Shandy was far from being her usual bright self. She hadn't probed the reason for Della's call, merely agreeing to come at ten o'clock as requested.

Della lived in a fashionable part of North Terrace, a tree-lined boulevard on the edge of the city centre. Shandy hadn't visited her before, so she was intrigued when the address turned out to be a charming nineteenth-century residence with a slate roof and shuttered bay windows. In front was a mossy paved courtyard with a lovely old gum tree as a centrepiece and a tall wrought-iron fence separating the property from the street.

The house had been divided into apartments, one to each floor, and a doorman showed her to an antique lift which creaked and groaned its way up to the top floor where Della lived.

Only as she reached for the door knocker, did Shandy hesitate. Della had said some cruel things to her about Russell. What if she wanted to taunt her afresh?

'Sticks and stones . . .' she reminded herself firmly and reached for the brass knocker, giving it a decisive rap against the door.

It was opened at once, suggesting that Della had been waiting for her, and Shandy drew an involuntary breath as she caught sight of the other woman. Della's shining platinum hair, normally impeccably groomed, was pulled back into a severe ponytail and her face was bare of make-up, the tell-tale lines of her age being fully revealed for the first time. Only her clothes reflected the familiar Della. Her navy slacks were beautifully tailored to show off her slim figure, while her youthful breasts were encased in a shell-pink crocheted top.

As she caught sight of Shandy she put a hand to her hair selfconsciously. 'Come in, please. I know I look a sight.'

'You look fine,' Shandy assured her, but privately she was worried. It must have taken a lot to persuade Della to appear before anyone in what, to her, was a state of disarray. Shandy couldn't remember ever seeing her with a hair out of place, or minus a full make-up. She realised she was staring and quickly transferred her gaze to the room into which she had been shown.

It seemed that Barbara must take after her mother, because the lovely antique furniture was draped with clothes and every table surface was littered with fashion magazines and jars of cosmetics. Della followed her glance around the room. 'You'll have to excuse the mess. It's my maid's day off.'

From Barbara, Shandy knew that Russell still made his ex-wife an allowance. From the look of the apartment, it must be generous indeed, especially if she could afford a maid. Still, no amount of money could compensate for what Della had given up, Shandy thought sadly. She turned to Della. 'Is Barbara here?'

'No. I . . . I thought it was better if we talked alone. Please sit down. Can I get you anything?'

'No thanks, I'm fine.' More than anything, she wanted to escape from Della's presence which was making her increasingly nervous. 'If it's about the paintings . . .'

Della seemed surprised. 'Paintings? Oh, those. They're at Clough's. Why?'

'Wasn't that why you asked me to come—to take them back?' Shandy asked, baffled.

To her horror, Della's face crumpled as if she was about to burst into tears. With an obvious effort, she regained control of herself. 'No. When we unpacked them, the committee was delighted with them and voted to put them straight into the exhibition. I . . . I couldn't do anything about it. If you really want them back, you'll have to see Conrad Clough at the Gallery. He's looking after everything for the committee. He liked your work, by the way.'

'I see. Then if it wasn't to fetch the paintings, why did you ask me to come?'

Della looked down at her hands as if seeing them for the first time. 'I acted very badly the other day,' she began awkwardly. 'I know what you must think of me.'

'You don't need to explain anything to me.'

She raised her eyes and again, Shandy saw the fear in them. 'Yes, I do. Barbara doesn't know any more than what I've told her.'

'If you're going to ask me not to say anything to her, I've already told you . . .'

'I know. But I'd feel better if you knew something of my side of the story.' The bitterness was evident in her voice as she said, 'I'm sure you already know Russell's version.'

Shandy jumped to her feet. 'I don't want to hear anyone's *version*,' she insisted. 'What happened between you and Russell is your own business and it's certainly none of mine.'

As she saw Della react with surprise, Shandy realised she had used Russell's first name with a casualness which could suggest long acquaintance. 'You've made it your business by getting involved with him,' Della told her.

It was worse than Shandy had feared. The only way she could disabuse Della of the idea that she was romantically interested in Russell was to tell her how she came to be at Chedoona Downs. And she couldn't do that without jeopardising Russell's chance of being reunited with his daughter. 'You're determined to think I'm having an affair with him, aren't you?' she asked heavily, sitting down again.

'What other conclusion can I draw?' Della asked, regaining some of her poise. 'Since he likes to play the art collector, doubtless you met him at some arty function or other and wasted no time introducing yourself as his daughter's dearest friend. He'd be only too glad to hear all about her progress from you—over coffee say, or was it dinner by then? I don't suppose it was very difficult to win him over. You're not unattractive, my dear.'

Shandy felt the colour drain from her face. How could Della suggest she would do anything so underhanded as to use her friendship with Barbara in such a vile manner? 'I don't have to listen to this,' she whispered.

'I'm afraid you do,' Della rapped out, catching Shandy offguard. Gone was all suggestion of the vulnerability she had displayed only moments before. 'Miss Giles is rather stuffy about how the girls on her books behave, I understand.'

'What are you saying?'

Della's eyes narrowed. 'I think you know. If she heard that one of her students had been bed-hopping with a man old enough to be her father, she might not be so keen on having that girl on her books.'

Shandy drew a sharp breath. 'You wouldn't dare!'

'I would dare a great deal, my dear, if I thought it would

protect my daughter.' All at once, the hard expression softened again, confusing Shandy so that she wondered whether she had heard Della's threat correctly. 'I don't want you to think I'm only worrying for myself,' Della said pleadingly, the vulnerability back in her face. 'It's not fair to make Barbara pay for my mistakes. I was very young—younger than you are now when I married Russell and had a child. I couldn't make Russell understand that I needed some freedom. He tried to manage me the way he'd managed his property.'

Her thoughts in turmoil, Shandy found herself privately agreeing with Della about Russell's attitude to people, even if she couldn't accept the other woman's reasoning. 'Why are you telling me all this?' she asked uncomfortably.

'I want you to understand that Russell's not the man for you. You'd only suffer the way I did, and I don't want to see that happen.'

You're also terrified in case Russell marries again and produces an heir to displace Barbara, Shandy thought dispassionately. Well, she had no cause to worry. Everything Della had told her only reinforced her own view of Russell as a man who enjoyed manipulating people. She might have made the mistake of falling in love with him, but her love was a flower which would quickly wilt if she starved it of light and air, as she intended to do. The pain which shafted through her at this thought would have to be endured until the infatuation wore off, as it must if she refused to encourage it.

She stood up. 'I think we understand each other,' she said levelly.

Relief lightened Della's features and she smiled thinly. 'I'm so glad. In years to come, you'll see I've done you a favour, my dear.'

Shandy started towards the door, but Della intercepted her and pushed a piece of paper into her hand. She looked at it, uncomprehending. 'What's this for?'

'It's a cheque . . . made out to Monica Giles,' Della said quickly as Shandy began to protest. 'I thought it would help if I paid your next term's fees.'

Shandy's fingers shook with anger as she methodically tore the cheque into pieces and handed them to Della. 'I told you I don't want your money, in any form.'

Shaken, she hurried out of the flat and took the stairs instead of the lift to give herself time to calm down before she emerged into the sunlight again. The nerve of the woman, first trying to blackmail her, then offering to buy her co-operation.

She was still fuming, but outwardly calm by the time she reached the Clough Gallery. It was located in an old colonial building with arched windows and Dutch gables in Kintore Avenue, not far from the Parliament House. The fact that the owner, Conrad Clough, had told Della he liked Shandy's work did not impress her at all. The Clough Gallery was a favourite establishment with the well-to-do, so Clough would be kind because he knew she was an acquaintance of the socially prominent Della Stratton.

The charity exhibition was in the main room and she located it easily, recognising her own work at once among the many paintings on show. Without more than glancing at them, she hurried through to the glass-walled office at the back of the gallery. A thin, balding man was working behind a desk, and he looked up as she approached. 'May I help you, Miss?'

'I'm looking for Conrad Clough.'

'Is there anything I can do to help?'

'I'm Shandy . . . er . . . Charlotte Farrer,' she began.

His smile widened. 'Ah yes, the talented Miss Farrer.'
He stood up and moved quickly round to her side of the
desk, holding out his hand. 'Delighted to meet you. I'm
Conrad Clough. I can't tell you how pleased I was with
your work. Now what can I do for you?'

'That's what I came about,' she said, suddenly nervous.
'My paintings were put into the exhibition by mistake. I
came to ask for them back.'

His smile was replaced by a look of annoyance, quickly
masked by professional conviviality. 'Well, it was a lucky
mistake for you, young lady.'

'Lucky? How could that be?'

'All your work was sold within the first two hours of the
exhibition opening.'

Her mouth dropped open. 'Sold? *All* of them?'

He seemed pleased by her reaction. 'All of them. Mr
Stratton was so thrilled with them.'

The elation which had begun to course through her was
immediately replaced by a cold sensation. 'Wait a minute.
You mean Russell Stratton was here, and bought all of my
paintings?'

'That's right. He called in this morning, as soon as he
read that I had a new exhibition. Luckily, he's in town for
a few days. He's been a customer of mine for years.' While
Shandy watched open-mouthed, he reached into his desk
and took out a cheque. 'This is for your share of the sale.
The balance goes to the charity and the gallery, of course,
but I think you'll find your share satisfactory.'

He handed the piece of paper to her and she took it
between two fingers, as if it could bite. The anger she had
been struggling to keep in check since the meeting with
Della, threatened to surface again. Conrad Clough took in
her strained expression. 'You don't seem very pleased
about the sale.'

'Is it any wonder, when they were bought as an act of charity?' she said bitterly.

His eyebrows arched questioningly. 'Well, I'm sure he was happy to help the less fortunate as part of the deal, but I can assure you the main reason he bought your pictures was because he liked them. I've known Mr Stratton for a long time and I've never known him to buy anything out of philanthropy. He's a charitable man, certainly, but he's also a very astute businessman. His acquisitions must first appeal to his own high standards and, if possible, also have investment value.'

'No doubt you're right,' she agreed tiredly. Conrad Clough wasn't to know that the charity she suspected Russell of supporting was herself. He thought she meant the one for whose benefit the show had been arranged. Well, Russell might not be a philanthropist, but she wouldn't put it past him to buy her paintings to try to make amends for keeping her prisoner at Chedoona Downs. After Della's attempt to buy her co-operation this morning, Russell's action was the last straw. It seemed that the Strattons were all alike. The only language they understood was money. 'You say Russell Stratton is staying in Adelaide at the moment?' she asked.

Conrad Clough nodded, visibly relieved that she was at last acting properly grateful. 'I presume you want to let him know how you feel face-to-face?'

'Oh yes,' she agreed fervently, 'that's exactly what I intend to do.'

Luckily, she still possessed the card he had thrust into her hand before she left Ceduna, and she checked the address on it. Russell's apartment was in a new high-rise block close to the central business district.

She forced herself to smile as she took her leave of Conrad Clough.

'If you have any other work on hand, I'd like to see it,' he told her. 'You're a very fortunate young lady to have attracted the attention of a wealthy patron like Mr Stratton.'

'Oh, I'm sure he thinks so too,' she said through clenched teeth. Before she could break down and tell the gallery owner what she really thought, she hurried outside and took several gulps of fresh air to steady herself.

Russell was too much! How dare he think he could buy her like that? The cheque in her handbag bothered her to such an extent it was all she could do not to tear it to shreds as she had done with Della's offering this morning. She reminded herself that it would be much more satisfying to throw it in Russell's face. How could she have been so foolish as to fall in love with someone so callous and unfeeling?

Unhappily, she sank down onto a park bench and stared unseeingly at the pigeons that clustered hopefully around her feet. She felt as if she was being torn in two. Half of her insisted on recalling the feel of Russell's hands on her skin, and the ravishing touch of his mouth on hers as he plundered her senses and carried her to heights of ecstasy she had never dreamed existed. The same errant part yearned to experience his touch again and ached for the fulfilment of his possession. That was the part she must fight with all the reason at her command. Because the other part of her recognised the danger he represented.

Della was right. Russell wouldn't marry a woman—he would buy her body and soul. The worldly goods with which he would endow his bride would turn out to be shackles, corrupting and destroying the way great wealth always did; the way it had destroyed her parents.

She had never felt the loss of her parents more acutely than she did at that moment. If only she could seek her mother's down-to-earth advice or her father's rough and ready, but always practical, counsel. But they were gone, killed by the windfall they had been so sure would solve all their problems. It had, in a way, she thought bitterly, but it had left her with a legacy which all the love in the world couldn't change.

Resolutely, she stood up amid a flurry of wings as the pigeons scattered in panic. She had better get it over with. The sooner she told Russell that she wouldn't accept his patronage, the sooner she would be free of him for good.

But did she really want to be free of him? She couldn't even answer that to her satisfaction. She only knew she had to convince him that he couldn't buy her, as he seemed to think he could.

Nevertheless, it took all the courage she possessed to make her way to the address on his card, and go inside to ask for him. The security guard manning the foyer of the luxurious building directed her to a bank of elevators, one of which would whisk her to Russell's floor.

She was trembling with anticipation by the time she reached his front door, and her hand shook when she reached for the bell push. Distantly, she heard chimes within the apartment, followed by footsteps coming towards her.

As they came closer, she almost turned and ran for the elevator, but it was too late. The door swung open and Russell stood framed in the opening. As she looked at him, her heart seemed to freeze into a painful lump in her chest and she felt as if she was suffocating. Had it only been a matter of days since she saw him last? Every muscle and sinew, every dark hair and character line was burned into her memory. She fought the urge to fling herself into his arms, remembering the reason why she was here.

'Shandy!' he said, pleasure in his voice. 'Clough must have told you I was in town.'

'That's right. I've just come from him,' she said, keeping her tone level with an effort. 'I've come to return something of yours.'

She thrust the cheque into his hands and turned to leave, but he caught her arm. 'What's this all about?'

'I'm sorry, it isn't the full amount you paid but some of it went to the charity and the gallery. This is the amount left for the other charity.'

He frowned impatiently. 'What other charity? You're not making any sense!'

'I'm the other charity—the one you thought you'd take care of with your generous gesture of buying up all my paintings.'

'What?' he exploded. 'I think you'd better come in while I try and straighten out this crazy idea of yours.'

The last thing she wanted was to spend any more time alone with him. 'No, I . . . I'm in a hurry,' she improvised.

'Oh no you don't. I want to know what this is all about, and you're not getting away until you tell me.' Her strength was no match for his, so she had no choice but to let herself be propelled into the foyer. Behind her, the door slammed shut with a hollow sound, reminding her that she was trapped. 'Through there,' he ordered peremptorily, gesturing towards a spacious living room beyond the foyer.

Timidly, she walked into the room and was confronted by a panoramic view of the city from picture windows which took up two walls of the lounge room. At her feet a sunken conversation area was furnished with leather couches piled with cushions. She skirted the pit with its suggested intimacy, and perched on the edge of a bar stool alongside the well-stocked bar.

Without asking, Russell went behind the bar and poured drinks for them both. Scotch, she noticed distastefully. He raised his glass to her in a silent toast, then downed the drink in one swallow. She ignored hers and waited tremulously for him to begin.

'Now, what in blazes is this all about?' he demanded. 'I do you a favour by buying your pictures, which were on public exhibition, by the way—and this is the thanks I get.'

'That's exactly the point I came here to make. I don't want you doing me any favours,' she stated.

'Perhaps I didn't put that very well. Would it help if I said I *liked* your work?'

That was what Conrad Clough had said. If only she could believe them! 'No, it wouldn't,' she demurred. 'I know you're trying to make amends for keeping me at Chedoona.'

He set his glass down with a crash. 'Damn it! I am not trying to make amends for anything, you stubborn female! The work is good, as good as any of Heysen's early works. In time, if you continue to progress, your work will be brilliant, so my purchases today were in the nature of an investment against that time.'

Again, she wished desperately that she could believe him. But by comparing her to Heysen, he had only convinced her that she was right. No matter how competent she might know herself to be, she wasn't in Heysen's league and probably never would be, so her work would never have the investment value Russell tried to claim. 'Nice try,' she said wryly. 'And I really appreciate you pandering to my ego like this, but there's no need. I know my own limitations.'

'Do you?' he said softly and his eyes bored into hers with disturbing intensity. 'Do you have any idea just what you're capable of, Shandy Farrer?'

'I . . . I don't know what you mean,' she said uneasily.

'Yes, you do. When we were stranded on the road to Chedoona, I got a glimpse of the true passion in your nature. You felt it too, although you're trying to pretend it never happened. Why do you keep running away like this?'

'No, I don't,' she defended herself.

'You're doing it now, this minute. You can't accept that I would buy your work on its own merits, because that would mean recognising your own talent, so you invent some phoney philanthropic motive which is easier to accept. Just as you'd rather tell yourself it's my money that scares you when you're really scared of admitting that you could love me.'

Tears sprang to her eyes as he touched a raw nerve. Hadn't she been saying much the same things to herself only a short time ago as she sat in the park? 'I hate you!' she hurled at him.

'No, you don't. Why can't you accept the truth?'

'It's you who can't accept it!' she flung back at him. She felt as if her very existence was in danger of being swamped by the force of his personality. She was sinking fast and if she didn't escape soon, it would be too late. The fact that she did love him made it all the more imperative that he didn't find out the truth. If he did, he would use it to bend her to his will and then she would be lost forever. 'I . . . I can't be in love with you,' she finished feebly.

'Why not? Because of this stupid money hang-up you have?'

She looked fixedly out at the view, anything to avoid having to meet his eyes. 'No, it's because—there's someone else.'

'A phantom lover, I suppose,' he said derisively.

She kept her tone calm, despite the pounding of her heart which threatened to burst from her chest at any minute. 'No, he's real enough. In fact, I've already mentioned his name to you.'

'Go on.'

'Jordan Cole.' The choice of name was impulsive and she hoped Jordan would forgive her for it. But she had to convince Russell that she wasn't in love with him and this was the only way she could devise.

To her astonishment, Russell laughed explosively. 'Ah, Shandy, full marks for trying. But you've overlooked how much trouble you went to to assure me that your involvement with Cole was strictly platonic.'

'And, of course, you believed me?'

For the first time, she saw doubt in his expression and she hated herself for putting it there. He had begun to trust her, probably the first time he had trusted any woman since Della betrayed him. Now Shandy would have to betray his trust all over again, and probably destroy for all time his last vestiges of faith in womankind.

His hand shook slightly as he poured himself another drink, but he left it on the bar. 'Are you telling me that there *is* something between you and Cole?'

She put all the conviction she could muster into her response. 'Of course there is. Why do you think I was so shattered when I couldn't get to Melrose to join him?'

'Shack up with him, don't you mean?' he interjected bitterly. 'Oh, don't wince so prettily. Obviously, your innocence is as much an act as that passionate display you put on for me at Ceduna.' Tiredly, he passed a hand across his eyes. 'It looks like I've made a bloody fool of myself all over again. When you responded so ardently in my arms, you were thinking of him all the time, weren't you?'

She nodded, too numb with misery to speak. The sad, disillusioned way he was looking at her was almost more than she could bear, but she could think of no way to ease his pain without betraying her true feelings.

He picked up his glass and drained it, then set it down carefully. 'Just as well I found out in time, wasn't it?'

'That's what I've been trying to tell you.'

'Yes, you have,' he agreed thoughtfully, 'except that I was reading your body instead of your words—that is, I thought I was reading your responses right, but I can't have been, because I never had you figured as a two-faced bitch. Della, yes—but never you.'

The calm, cold way he said it shocked her. 'Just because you made a mistake, there's no need to assassinate my character,' she said hotly.

'No, I suppose there isn't. But I'm damned if I'll apologise. You led me on—I wasn't wrong about that. What baffles me is why? What did you hope to gain?' His eyes widened in sudden understanding. 'Della,' he breathed, 'she put you up to this, didn't she?'

'No!'

'Of course, somehow she found out that I wanted to have Barbara brought to Ceduna and arranged for you to take her place. That's it, isn't it?'

'Oh for heaven's sake, that's too preposterous for words!'

'Is it? Not from my point of view. It's just the sort of despicable trick Della would pull to keep me away from Barbara and make a fool of me at the same time.'

How could he have arrived at such an outrageous conclusion? All she had wanted to do by coming here was to put an end to any future involvement between herself and Russell. She had certainly achieved that, but in a way she had never expected. Now he hated her, not only because he thought she was in love with someone else, but because he thought she was Della's pawn and had been a willing party to an attempt to discredit him. 'You've got it all wrong,' she said miserably.

'No, I don't think so. It all fits too neatly. I'm surprised the thought never occurred to me before.' He laughed harshly. 'You're in the wrong profession, my dear. Instead of being an artist, you should be an actress.' He thought for a moment, 'Just tell me one thing. Was Barbara a party to your little scheme?'

'No!' she denied vehemently. 'That is . . . there isn't any scheme, as you call it. You have the most devious mind of any man I've ever met.'

'That's quite a compliment coming from an expert in the art.'

The tears which had been lingering at the back of her eyes threatened to spill over at any minute. If she didn't get away from here soon, she would break down completely. In her present vulnerable state, it would be too easy to tell him how much she really loved him. After the scene they had just played out, there was no way he would believe her, and she couldn't bear it if he mocked her love for him. Keeping her face averted, she swung the stool around and stumbled off it, but he caught at her arm.

'Wait a minute. You've forgotten this.'

He was holding out the cheque she had returned to him and she shook her head decisively. 'Keep it. I meant it when I said I didn't want it.'

'Not even as a memento of me?'

'No,' she said huskily. Especially not that.

'Then you'd better have something else to remember me by,' he said quietly.

She stared at him, her tears momentarily averted. 'What do you mean?'

'This.'

Before she realised what he meant to do, he took her into his arms, pinning her hands by her sides so that she was unable to resist. Then he covered her mouth with his own, forcing her lips apart and invading her mouth with his tongue. Something exploded in her brain and her lips parted willingly under his, so that he no longer had to fight her. She knew he meant to punish her for betraying him, but she didn't care. His kiss would be a memento of him, one she would cherish all her days. As his lips roved over her face and throat, she dropped her head back and closed her eyes. Her breath was fast and shallow in her throat as a fiery sensation began in her loins and surged up the length of her body. His hold on her arms slackened and of their own volition, her arms crept up to wind themselves around his neck, drawing him even closer against her.

God, how she loved him. How could anything else matter but this? Surely everything else could be solved if only they could cling to this wondrous shared passion. She opened her mouth to tell him so, but before she could speak, he thrust her away from him.

'Russell, I . . .'

'Spare me any more fairy tales,' he said wearily. 'I just wanted you to have something to remember me by when you're rolling in the hay with your boyfriend. Maybe then, instead of kissing me and pretending it was him as you were doing at Chedoona, you'll be kissing him and wishing it was me. Because I'm damned sure he can't arouse you the way I can. Some things you can't fake, even if all else is a lie. That will be your punishment, Shandy Farrer. Now get the hell out of my life.'

Blinded by the tears which refused to be held back any longer, she groped her way to the front door and did as he ordered.

CHAPTER NINE

NEXT day, Shandy awoke with a heavy, lethargic feeling. At first, she couldn't recall what was so terribly wrong; then it came flooding back and she turned her face into the pillow in anguish. Russell had told her to get out of his life forever.

Wasn't that what she wanted? she asked herself. On the surface it was, but deep down she wasn't so sure. He had asked her to accept that she could love him, but what good would that do her since there was no future in their relationship? Maybe she had bruised his precious ego by refusing to acknowledge her love for him. If he was so insecure that he needed endless declarations of love from every female who crossed his path, it was hardly her fault. He had to find out sometime that not every woman he met was prepared to swoon at his feet.

'Damn, damn, damn!' she muttered aloud, flinging back the bedcovers. Who was she kidding? Certainly not herself. It wouldn't have taken much to have her swooning at his feet with the best of them, if she thought there was any chance at all for them. But their philosophies of life were too much at odds with each other.

Added to which, she was hurt beyond measure by his accusation that she had conspired with Della against him. She sighed deeply. She felt like a tennis ball which had been batted back and forth between Russell and Della. Once more, she wished she was back in her parents' suburban cottage where a marriage lasted 'till death us do part' and life was so much less complicated.

'Life doesn't allow us to go back,' Russell had told her. He was right about that at least. Somehow, she had to make up her mind to go forward from here—if only she knew how . . . and forward to what?

One thing she did know—she couldn't go back to the Academy tomorrow and pretend that all was well. Facing Barbara would be bad enough, although she was sure she could make her friend see the foolishness of Della's accusations. What she felt totally unable to do was parade before the other girls with a falsely bright expression and happy smile. If she tried, she knew her face would crack like a statue's.

So what was she going to do?

A sudden inspiration made her smile for the first time in days. Why not make her lie to Russell into a partial truth, and go to the Flinders Ranges for a while? If she could spend a little time at the Melrose colony with Jordan Cole, she might be able to straighten out her tangled life somehow. Surely Jordan, of all people, would understand her plight and have some sage advice to offer her.

Suiting the action to the thought, she snatched up the telephone and dialled the number of the Giles Academy. The cultured accents of the receptionist answered.

'Is Miss Giles there?' she asked.

'Monica Giles here,' came the response a few moments later.

Hesitantly, Shandy explained that she had some pressing personal problems which would prevent her returning to the Academy right away.

'If there's anything I can do to help . . .' Miss Giles began, but Shandy forestalled her.

'No, thank you. I just need a week or so to sort myself . . . that is . . . to sort everything out.'

There was a pause as Monica Giles digested this. 'I see. You do intend to come back, I take it?'

'Oh yes, of course.' She had never considered anything else.

Miss Giles sounded relieved. 'I'm so glad. You know I don't dispense praise over-generously,' (that was the understatement of the year, Shandy thought), 'but I do regard you as one of my most promising young models.'

'Thank you, Miss Giles. I'll see you in a week.' Thoughtfully, she replaced the phone. It was the first time Monica Giles had called her a model instead of a student, and she found the unaccustomed praise comforting. Her personal life might be in ruins but at least she was good for something.

She still had the problem of how to get herself up to the Flinders Ranges.

'Of course you can borrow my car,' her neighbour, Sarah, told her as soon as she raised the question. Her pretty round face was wreathed in smiles. 'I *knew* there was something between you and Jordan Cole. Why else would you be pining away down here until you can get back to see him again?'

Shandy sighed. What was the use? 'You're an incurable romantic,' she told Sarah. 'Are you sure you won't miss the car?'

'Tom's away at an engineering conference interstate, so I have the use of his air-conditioned Commodore,' she explained. 'It's bliss to drive after my temperamental little Marina. I hope you won't find the gears too much of a handful.'

'I'll manage. I wish I could afford a car of my own.'

'The only reason we have two is because Tom needs his for his work, but they are costly to run,' Sarah agreed. 'We may even give up the Marina soon, because I won't be able to fit behind the wheel much longer.'

Shandy looked at her neighbour speculatively, and Sarah nodded shyly. 'You guessed it—I'm pregnant.'

Impulsively, Shandy hugged her. 'Congratulations! Is Tom happy about it?'

'Over the moon. We've wanted a child for ages, but it just didn't work out. Then just when we decide to give up . . . presto!'

'Why does it always seem to work like that? You want something in life so much it hurts, but you don't get it until you stop going after it?' Shandy said pensively.

Sarah laughed. 'My, you are getting philosophical! I've a feeling there's a moral in that somewhere, but I'm too obtuse to work it out. So let's get down to more practical matters. When will you want the car?'

'This morning, if I may. It's about a four-hour drive, so if I leave mid-morning, I can be at Melrose before the shops close, buy some provisions and go straight out to Orana before dark.'

'My, my, such haste—and you tell me there's nothing between you and Jordan!'

'Sarah, you're impossible!'

Despite Shandy's protestations, her friend's good-natured teasing had been just the tonic she needed to rouse her out of her lethargy. She was feeling much better by the time she climbed into Sarah's battered white Marina and set off for the Flinders. It hadn't taken her very long to pack, although she felt a brief pang as she folded her checked shirt and jeans into a rucksack. They were the same clothes she had worn at Chedoona Downs and the memories they aroused threatened her fragile good mood.

Only by concentrating on the driving—which was easy enough to do since she found the unfamiliar gears every bit as temperamental as Sarah had warned—was she able to dispel her gloom, at least for the moment.

Her mood lightened even more as she gradually left the city behind and began to climb towards the scenic splendour of the Flinders Ranges. During the two-hundred-mile drive, she stopped only once for a hamburger lunch at a roadside eatery, then pressed on, anxious to reach the Orana colony before dark.

It was late afternoon by the time she reached Melrose, the nearest town to the colony, and the oldest settlement in the Ranges. Even the few tourists who wandered the streets couldn't disturb its atmosphere of brooding tranquillity.

She greeted the pioneer buildings like the old friends they were. The old police station and courthouse was now a museum, but it was easy to imagine it as the centre of law and order it had once been. The mill and the blacksmith's shop now catered for tourists, but had been vital centres in their day. Like the charming pioneer cottages, they looked as if a tough old settler might emerge from one of them at any moment.

Several local people recognised her from earlier visits and greeted her with typical country warmth. However, she stopped only long enough to stock the car with provisions—bacon, eggs, crusty fresh bread, milk, cheese and an assortment of tinned goods—before following the track along the creek towards Orana.

Mindful that she was driving a borrowed car, she manoeuvred carefully over the rutted track. Around her, the solitude of the bush was awesome as she drove between the magnificent Red River gums which lined the creek on one side, and the forest of casuarinas, native

pines and wattles which clothed the valleys and clung to
hills and rock crevices on the other side.

As she reached the flat-rock fence which bordered
Orana, she braked sharply and, on impulse, turned off the
engine, letting the stillness of the bush close over her. She
had been right to come here.

Orana was deserted when she drove up to the cluster of
buildings which made up the colony. 'Anybody here?' she
called, hearing her voice echo back at her from the distant
hills. There was no answer. They were probably scattered
through the bush, working, she decided. She started to
unpack the car, transferring her things to one of the
bunkrooms and stowing the provisions in the communal
kitchen.

Orana was built around the remains of a homestead
dating back to the 1850s. The eighteen-inch-thick walls
were made from flat rocks taken from the nearby creek
bed, and stacked ingeniously on top of one another
without the need for mortar. Like any such early
dwellings, the main room had no communicating doors
to the bedrooms, so after an evening around the fireside, it was often a chilly trip outside to reach the bedrooms.

For this reason she had chosen a bedroom close to the
main room, and was surprised to find there were no signs
of other occupants. That was odd, since people came and
went at Orana all the year round, and there were usually a
dozen or so artists in residence. Jordan had built two large
timber-pole structures near the main dwelling, to provide
additional accommodation for visitors.

When the sun set and there was still no sign of anyone,
she began to worry in earnest. What if everyone had left
for some reason? What if Jordan wasn't here after all?
Perhaps she should have telephoned Melrose to check

instead of just coming up here, although she had never needed to check ahead before.

Anxiously, she hurried outside and screamed as she came hard up against a muscular figure. 'Jordan!'

He held her at arm's length. 'Shandy—it *is* you!'

Never had she been so pleased to see anyone as she was to see his tall, commanding figure in front of her. In appearance he was a modern-day Viking, with thick, curling blonde hair, a suggestion of blonde moustache, and a tall, lithe figure which would have looked at home on the deck of a Long Ship. She leaned against him for support and allowed herself to be steered into the main room, her heart still pounding erratically. 'You gave me such a fright just now.'

He grinned wryly. 'I gave *you* a fright? What about me? I leave the place apparently deserted, and come back to find a wood-nymph in residence. What are you doing here, by the way?'

'The usual,' she said evasively. 'I came up to paint—and to get away for a while.'

'Then you haven't heard?'

'Heard what?' she asked uneasily.

'I'm closing Orana. The land is wanted for a national park, so I've agreed to sell. I'm moving the colony to a new location north of Blinman, in the Ranges proper.'

The idea of Orana closing was so unthinkable, she stared at him in disbelief. 'Can't . . . can't you refuse to sell?' she asked unsteadily.

'I'm quite glad about it, actually. Civilisation is catching up with us here, so I'd rather be less accessible. Don't look so stricken—you'll love the new location.'

At any other time she would have agreed with him, but her emotions were too close to the surface for rational thinking. All she could absorb was that the place she had thought of as a refuge for so long would soon be closed to her. On top of everything else, it was almost more than she could bear. To her horror, tears began to course down her cheeks and she found, once she started to cry, she was unable to stop.

Jordan crossed the room in two strides and took her in his arms. 'Here, none of that! I didn't think you'd take it so hard.'

'B-but I l-love it here,' she sobbed.

'Even so, nothing stays the same forever. Everything changes, you know that.'

She did know it, but it was still the wrong thing to say, and her sobs became even more heart-rending. Sensing the depths of her desolation, Jordan held her close to him and rested her head on his chest, muttering meaningless platitudes to her in an undertone as he stroked the damp hair back from her forehead. At last, the sobs subsided and she struggled to sit upright. 'I'm sorry,' she said abjectly.

'For being human? Don't apologise, love. Life gets too much for everyone occasionally. But it wasn't just this place closing, was it? You were acting as if your heart was broken, and no piece of real estate could do that.'

'You're right,' she confessed. 'But I'd rather not talk about it now, if you don't mind.' If she did, she would dissolve into tears again.

He shrugged. 'Suit yourself, love. Anyway, the move won't happen overnight, so you're welcome to stay here for a week or so, at least until you sort out whatever's bothering you.'

She smiled at him through a veil of tears. 'Thanks, Jordan. Whatever would I do without you?'

He overruled her protests and insisted on making supper for them both, although he did agree to use the provisions she had brought. He went to work in the kitchen, which was part of the main room, separated from it by a line of low cupboards. Soon the air was redolent with the smell of frying bacon and an omelette fragrant with fresh herbs.

'Wine for m'lady?' he asked, producing a bottle with a flourish.

'I didn't bring any wine,' she laughed.

'Just because we believe in going back to nature here, doesn't mean we need abandon civilisation altogether,' he said, laughing. 'I raided my very private cellar for this label.'

Since it was a rare vintage from a famous Barossa Valley vineyard, she raised an eyebrow. 'You must have quite a cellar.'

He grinned boyishly, revealing twin rows of perfect white teeth which contrasted with the tanned smoothness of his skin. 'Oh, I'm quite a guy all round.'

She couldn't argue about that and it crossed her mind how pleasant it would be if she really *was* in love with Jordan Cole. She had loved him, in a fashion, ever since she had attended his art classes in Adelaide when she was sixteen, but it was the kind of love she imagined she would have had for a brother if she'd had one. Sarah would be shattered to hear her thinking like this, she knew, but she couldn't help how she felt.

Over dinner, they talked about an exhibition they'd both attended in Adelaide, and about various people they both knew. Jordan seemed to sense her need to steer away from personal subjects, and accommodated her with his usual unfailing charm.

Only when they reached the coffee stage, did he touch her arm lightly. 'Are you sure you're all right?'

She nodded. 'I'm fine now.' She let him lead her away

from the table, to a pile of cushions stacked in front of the massive fireplace. Someone had told her it was big enough to roast a whole steer, but no-one had ever tried it to her knowledge. Now she settled herself on the cushions and stared at the dancing flames.

Without any conscious design, she relaxed against him and her head dropped back against his broad shoulder. Only when his lips brushed the top of her hair did she become fully aware of his nearness. His breath was a warm breeze on her cheek and in her somnolent state, she found the sensation pleasing. Unconsciously, she tilted her face up to his.

His breathing quickened, and all at once, he bent over her and claimed her mouth in a sweet, persuasive kiss. In all the time she had known Jordan it was the first time he had kissed her and it was so unexpected that she responded.

Gradually, his kiss became more demanding and she felt the rising level of his excitement as his lean body pressed against hers. As the warmth of his lips on hers increased, she searched for an answering passion in herself but, to her dismay, found none. With a curious sense of detachment, she felt Jordan's hand slide inside her blouse and caress the soft fulness of her breasts. She did not resist because she did love him in a way, but there was no matching fire coursing through her veins such as she could sense in him.

'Shandy, you're beautiful,' he breathed thickly.

Guiltily, she tried to pull away, but he held her against him. 'Jordan, I . . .'

'It's all right,' he said softly, 'I'll be gentle with you.'

She knew he would, and with all her heart, she wished she could respond to him as ardently as he wanted her to. Yet as he kissed her again, she heard an echo of Russell's parting words to her. 'You'll be kissing him and wishing it was me . . . he can't arouse you the way I can. That will be your punishment, Shandy Farrer.'

It was as if he had put some kind of curse on her because, try as she might, she couldn't get the image of Russell out of her mind. His mocking smile haunted her even as Jordan tried unsuccessfully to coax a response from her. She lay limply in his arms and finally, he hauled himself up on one elbow. 'It's no good, is it?'

'No, I'm afraid not. I'm sorry, Jordan . . .'

Gently, he teased the edges of her lips with his fingers. 'Will you stop apologising? I can tell when I don't turn a woman on—and you're about as turned-off as anyone I've ever encountered.'

'I'm so . . .' she began, and smiled. 'I nearly said it again.'

'But you didn't, so we're making progress, even if it's not the kind I had in mind. Maybe I'm the one who should say "sorry" for taking advantage of you when you're obviously vulnerable.'

'It wasn't entirely your fault,' she said. 'I wish it could be different between us, Jordan. I do love you in a way. I guess I always have. But not . . . not in that way.'

'There's someone else?'

She nodded. 'Not that it will do me any good.'

'Like that, is it? I should have guessed there was a man involved from the way you were acting earlier. What's the matter—is he married?'

'I wish it was as simple as that. No, we just don't see eye to eye about anything important. He doesn't trust women—including me, and I don't trust myself in his high-powered world.'

Jordan knew about the tragedy that had claimed her parents, and he nodded sympathetically. 'Sounds pretty hopeless,' he concurred. 'So you decided to come up here for some R & R?'

What an apt way to put it! Rest for her physical self and recuperation for her spirit, she reflected. 'That's about it,' she agreed.

He uncoiled from the cushions and stretched luxuriously. 'Well, I'm glad you've come clean. At least now I'll know enough to leave you alone while you're here.'

Her smile was warm and genuine, filled with all the sisterly love she bore for him. 'Thanks, Jordan, I knew you'd understand.'

He winked and faked an American accent. 'Here's looking at you, kid.'

She spent the next few days trying to immerse herself in work. On the northern side of the colony, along the banks of Campbell's Creek, were some of the finest River gums in the Ranges. They had been painted and sketched by countless artists before her, but each time she came to Orana she found some new perspective on the scene, and it was a challenge trying to translate it into paint.

This time, however, her heart wasn't in the attempt and she tore the sheet of sketching paper from the pad and crumpled it up in a ball to join the growing pile at her feet.

A shadow fell across the pad and she looked up to find Jordan standing over her. He regarded the litter of paper. 'Having problems?'

'Looks like it, doesn't it? I've never known it to be so elusive before.'

He frowned. 'Maybe you're trying too hard. Tell you what, why don't you come hiking with me? Perhaps some hard physical exercise will loosen up your sketching hand.'

Anything was worth a try, so she returned to her bunkroom, where she exchanged her sneakers for stout walking shoes. She debated whether to take her sketch block with her but decided Jordan might be right, she could be trying too hard. A few hours away from her work might be all she needed.

But even as she reasoned with herself, a small voice inside told her no amount of exercise would compensate for what really ailed her. Until she could exorcise the demon of Russell Stratton from her heart and mind, she would have very little peace of any kind.

In Jordan's jeep, they drove the few miles to Wilmington, north of the colony, then left the car at the southern end of the small town and set off on foot down the dirt road leading to Alligator Gorge

There were steps let into the side of the gorge and they climbed down these, between the towering cliffs which in some places were little more than the height of a man apart. At the bottom, they sheltered in the welcome shade of a eucalypt while Shandy regained her breath.

'You're out of condition,' Jordan chided her. 'How can you be fit for love if you aren't fit for anything else?'

Turning her head away, she pretended to be engrossed in the view down the gorge so that he wouldn't see the tears which sprang to her eyes at his words. He hadn't meant to be unkind, but he had touched a tender spot. She wasn't fit for love—not of the kind offered by a man like Russell, and she didn't feel fit for anything else either. But Jordan couldn't know the direction her thoughts took, so she chased the tears from her eyes with a shake of her head, and forced herself to smile at him. 'I'll show you who's out of condition,' she jeered. 'How far down the gorge do you want to go?'

'Show-off!' grinned Jordan. 'I've got a good mind to say Mambray Creek Park, for your cheek. But I'll let you off lightly since you're in such low spirits.' So he *had* seen her expression before she turned away. 'We'll just admire the scenery down here, pay homage to Camel Rock, then brace ourselves for the climb back up.'

Camel Head Rock was a dominant feature of Alligator Gorge and was named for its unmistakable resemblance to a camel, down to the eye and nostril visible in the layered rock. Along the bottom of the spectacular chasm, ferns grew in glorious profusion and elongated eucalypts made valiant attempts to reach the sky from the bed of the gorge. Despite her gloomy frame of mind, Shandy revelled in the fresh air with its myriad outdoor scents. Once she looked up and saw a wedge-tailed eagle hovering on the air currents atop the gorge. She envied the bird its freedom, both from the cares of humans, and to come and go as it pleased.

Jordan followed her thoughtful gaze. 'Wishing you could join him?'

'Can you imagine how free he must feel?'

'Free from some of our worries perhaps, but he's got a whole set of his own, don't forget. Hunters taking pot-shots at him, finding enough food to sustain him—no refrigerators in the sky; and these days, he's even got a problem finding a mate.'

She sighed. Why did it always come back to that? Poor wedge-tailed eagle. There were so few of them, she hadn't thought how lonely he must be or how difficult it would be to find an unattached female, as his instincts drove him to. But at least he didn't have to cope with the duplicity of men, she thought savagely. When he found his lady eagle, it would simply be a matter of doing what came naturally—no divorces, no scheming for him. Trust and fidelity would be a natural part of their relationship.

At lunchtime, they found a rock pool ringed by drab-coloured ti-trees, and sat in a patch of shade to eat the fruit

Jordan had provided. Afterwards, he dozed off to sleep, pulling his hat down low over his eyes. She had too much on her mind to sleep, so she occupied herself watching the birds which swooped down to enjoy the cool glades of the mirror-surfaced pool. High overhead, a flock of white cockatoos kept up a raucous chorus, and every now and then there would be a flash of iridescent green as a parrot swooped down to drink, then darted away. The tiny zebra finches were the most frequent visitors as they came down to drink and catch insects which they carried back to their nests high up on the cliff face.

The sun was low in the sky by the time Jordan stirred. He looked at his watch in surprise. 'Why didn't you waken me?'

'There didn't seem to be any hurry. Besides, I had a lot of thinking to do.'

He looked at her keenly. 'Did you reach any conclusions?'

'Not yet, but I think I'm getting there.' The tranquillity of the setting and its distance from people and their problems had greatly comforted her. Whether it had helped her to come to terms with her love for Russell, she wasn't yet sure. Maybe nothing could do that. But if it helped her to accept what she couldn't change, then it had been worthwhile.

'You do seem lighter in spirit,' Jordan commented as they ate together by the fireside at Orana that evening. This time she had insisted on doing the cooking and had turned the basic ingredients of pastry, eggs, bacon and chives snipped from a patch outside the door into a creditable quiche Lorraine. Jordan had produced another of his bottles of excellent wine to accompany the food. They finished the meal with crisp Jonathan apples and wedges of the Edam cheese she had brought.

'I do feel better,' she agreed. 'But if I keep eating like this, I'll go back pounds heavier.'

'It wouldn't do you any harm. When are you planning to go back, by the way?'

'I . . . I hadn't decided,' she said nervously. 'You're not throwing me out, are you?'

'I told you, you can take your time,' he assured her. 'But you'll have to stop running away some time.'

His words reminded her uncomfortably of what Russell had also said to her. He had accused her of running away from her own feelings. 'Men!' she said crossly. 'I do wish you'd stop trying to read my mind for me.'

'I wasn't reading your mind,' Jordan corrected quietly. 'I was judging by something far more revealing.'

'What . . . what are you getting at?'

'Your work. In class, I used to warn you how much your paintings revealed of your inner feelings?'

'Yes,' she agreed cautiously.

'Have you looked at the stuff you've done since you got here?'

'Of course I have. I didn't paint it blindfolded,' she retorted.

He was unperturbed by the derision in her voice. 'That's not what I meant and you know it. Come here.'

He held out his hand to her and after a moment's hesitation she slipped hers into it. 'Where are we going?'

'To look into Charlotte Farrer's mind,' he said cryptically.

Still holding her by the hand, he led her outside, and she gasped at the chill in the night air after the warmth of the fireside. His hand moved around her shoulders and he drew her close to him so that she was warmed by his body heat. Automatically, she stiffened at the contact. 'Relax,' he told her, 'we're just going to the studio.'

The studio was a cavernous stone building which had been the homestead's shearing shed. Inside, Jordan snapped on a light and closed the door behind them. Around the walls were ranged all the sketches and half-finished paintings she had worked on since she came to Orana. She stared at them, not sure what he expected of her.

'What do you think of them?' he asked.

'I . . . I don't know,' she stammered. 'They're not very good, I suppose.'

'You suppose right,' he said grimly. 'And I'll tell you why—your heart isn't in them. But it *is* in these.'

He led her across to the opposite wall where he had lined up sone of the sketches she had done at Chedoona and out on the Nullarbor.

'Where did you get those?' she asked.

'From your portfolio. I imagine you plan to translate them into paintings at some stage?'

'I . . . I already have.' They were the paintings which Russell had bought at the charity exhibition. She felt a sudden surge of fury at Jordan for displaying them like this. 'You had no right to go snooping among my things!'

'I wasn't snooping, as you call it,' he said evenly. 'We don't have locks on anything at Orana. I wanted to find out what was eating you—and help if I could.'

'You aren't helping by showing me these,' she said tearfully. 'I never want to see them again.'

'Or him?' he asked gently.

She gasped as he unrolled the portrait of Russell as his pirate ancestor. The sight of him constricted her heart painfully.

Jordan nodded knowingly as he rolled the picture up again. 'So he's the man you're in love with.'

'I'm not—I hate him!' she said vehemently.

'You hate him so much that you carry his picture

around the country with you?' He reached for her and she allowed herself to be enfolded in his comforting arms. 'Why don't you go back and try to make it up with him?' he urged.

'I c-can't. He told me to get out of his life forever.'

Jordan put his hand under her chin and tilted her tear-streaked face up to his. 'That doesn't mean you have to get out of *life* forever.'

'N-no, I suppose not.'

He seemed satisfied. 'Then you'll go home to Adelaide and start living again?'

She nodded. 'I'll try.'

He dropped a light kiss on her forehead. 'That's all anybody can do,' he told her.

CHAPTER TEN

SAFE in the circle of Jordan's arms, it had been easy enough to say she would try to rejoin the living. Actually doing it proved to be much more difficult, as she found when she returned to Adelaide and tried to pick up the pieces of her life.

If Sarah was surprised that she had come home alone, one look at Shandy's wan face and strained expression warned her that this was not the time to probe.

Instead, when Shandy dropped in to return her car keys and thank her for the loan of the car, Sarah put the kettle on. 'What you need is a good cup of tea,' she said as she deliberately prattled on about the coming baby and her plans to turn a spare bedroom into a nursery. 'You have such a marvellous eye for colour, you must give me some guidance on what scheme to choose for the baby,' she said.

Shandy grimaced. 'You're looking at someone who couldn't even choose what shirt to wear this morning—or whether to get up and get dressed at all.'

'That bad, huh?'

'Worse. Oh Sarah, I didn't know being in love could be so . . . so debilitating!'

Her neighbour nodded in understanding. 'Take it from one who's been there. It's rarely all moonlight and roses, even when you're as much in love as Tom and me. I still pine like a lovesick teenager whenever he's interstate on a job—which accounts for half our married life.' She covered Shandy's hand with her own. 'I gather things didn't work out so well between you and Jordan.'

Puzzled, Shandy stared at her, then realised that Sarah still thought she was in love with Jordan Cole. 'Everything's fine between Jordan and me. It always was.'

'Then why the long face?'

For a moment, she debated whether to tell Sarah the whole sad story, then decided against it. Firstly it would be unfair to burden her neighbour when she had enough to do worrying about the baby, and secondly she didn't want to bring Della and Barbara into it, which she would have to do if the story was to make any sense to a third party. 'It's too long and complicated,' she said. 'Besides, I think I'm on the mend now.'

Sarah looked relieved. 'I'm glad to hear it. Tom and I have been worried about you lately. Just remember, if ever you do feel like talking about it, I'm a terrific listener.'

'Thanks,' Shandy said fervently, 'you don't know how much that means to me. Since . . . since Mum and Dad died, there hasn't been anybody I could really talk to.'

'What else are friends for?' Sarah demanded, placing her hands on her hips as if she expected Shandy to argue. Her point made, she relaxed. 'By the way, how's Barbara? I haven't seen her around lately, and I thought she'd be back from Noumea by now.'

Shandy stirred her tea slowly. 'She is. Her mother thought she'd be better off living with her, than staying here.' That was close enough to the truth, she decided.

Sarah frowned worriedly. 'But how will you manage without someone to share the expenses?'

Shandy had been asking herself the same thing. The apartment was far too expensive for her to maintain alone, but she hated the idea of sharing with a stranger. 'I suppose I'll have to move out and find myself a bed-sitter I can afford,' she said.

Her neighbour looked downcast. 'Oh, Shandy, what

a shame. You were so happy living here. I know I'll certainly miss you if you have to move.'

'Thanks for saying so. But I don't know what else I can do.'

Sarah sipped her tea reflectively, then brightened. 'You could get a job. You told me you're nearly through that modelling course of yours. Surely if you had a word with whoever's in charge, they would let you start work straight away.'

It was an idea Shandy had considered herself, but she couldn't imagine Monica Giles being very enthusiastic.

'She doesn't have to be enthusiastic,' Sarah stated. 'She just has to agree.'

Obviously, Sarah had no inkling of how jealously Miss Giles guarded her agency's standards. She was always muttering about the appalling way she said some girls called themselves models after five minutes in front of a camera.

'Look at that!' she would say scathingly, as the girls studied videotapes of television commercials during their training. 'Her body is angled all wrong to do justice to the cut of that suit. And see how that one has her legs splayed out like a newborn calf.'

There was no way a Giles model would get away with such sloppy work, which was why they were in constant demand as cover girls, house models and parading collections for the country's leading fashion designers.

So Shandy was all the more surprised that Miss Giles even agreed to consider her request when she screwed up her courage and went to ask her about it next day.

'It's most irregular, you understand?' she said firmly.

'I know, Miss Giles, and I wouldn't have asked if it wasn't so important.'

The haughty lines of the former model's face softened

briefly. 'I know, Charlotte. And I admire the way you've managed your affairs until now. It can't have been easy for you, with your parents gone.' She thought for a moment. 'Would it help if I waived your last term fees?'

'That's very generous of you, Miss Giles, but I couldn't accept. I have to start paying my own way sometime, so I may as well start now.'

'So your mind is made up?'

'I'm afraid so,' Shandy agreed unhappily.

'Then there's nothing for it but to put you on the books right away,' Miss Giles said decisively.

'Oh, thank you so much,' Shandy smiled. 'It means so much to me . . .'

Miss Giles held up a restraining hand. 'Don't thank me yet,' she cautioned. 'I just don't want you signing with anyone else, but you'll have to start at the bottom with the hack jobs. You won't be a cover girl for quite a while yet.'

'I know that, of course. I'll tackle any assignment . . .'

'I hope you don't regret saying that,' Miss Giles said dourly. 'We'll see if you feel so starry-eyed after a spell of department store promotions and shopping centre tours.'

At that moment, Shandy wouldn't have cared if she was asked to dress up as a Red Indian and stand outside a tobacco store, holding cigars. As she completed the employment formalities with Miss Giles, she let her mind dwell on the future for the first time in days. At least there was now some brightness in the gloom. She would be able to keep the flat and feed herself, keeping what little remained of her parents' legacy in the bank as a nest-egg. In time, she might even get over this awful, dragging feeling which had haunted her ever since that final confrontation with Russell.

She still had nightmares about being aboard a Greek schooner in mid-ocean, but now the pirate captain was forcing her onto a plank suspended over the side of the ship with nothing but the fathomless depths underneath.

'Get the hell out of my life!' he ordered her. She had no choice but to walk out on to the plank, feeling it shudder beneath her at each step. Then his sword caught her in the small of the back and she went tumbling down and down, into the murky depths, as his mocking laughter echoed around her. She couldn't even scream because of the water closing over her head. Then she would awake, sweating and struggling in her bed.

She had told Sarah she was on the mend, but was she? As long as her dreams were haunted by him like this, what hope did she have of leading anything like a normal life?

She looked up as Miss Giles came back into the office with some forms in her hands. 'I've had them all witnessed, so everything is in order,' she told Shandy. 'Welcome to the Giles Agency, my dear.'

She shook hands formally with Miss Giles. 'Thank you for giving me this chance. I won't let you down.'

'If I thought you might, I wouldn't have given it to you,' Miss Giles told her tartly. 'You're to call in every morning at eight to check with the booking secretary. She'll tell you what assignments you have coming up.'

'I'll do that,' Shandy promised. She turned to leave, then had another thought, 'By the way, may I ask how Barbara Stratton is doing this term? She . . . she moved back home with her mother and I haven't heard from her since then.'

'That makes two of us,' Miss Giles said, to Shandy's surprise. 'She didn't come back to the Academy this term, even though her fees were paid in advance. Since she hasn't done me the courtesy of explaining, I'm afraid I can't help you.'

Puzzled, Shandy left the Academy. She couldn't imagine why Barbara would have given up her course so suddenly, especially without explaining to Monica Giles. Barbara had been so keen on becoming a model and Della had been equally pleased to have her daughter accepted by the most prestigious agency in Adelaide. So it wasn't likely that Della would have ordered Barbara to leave the Academy. It didn't make sense. Still, she wasn't going to add another Stratton's worries to her list, Shandy resolved. Between them, they had managed to leave her emotions in shreds, so whatever had prompted Barbara to give up her lifelong ambition would have to remain her own affair.

Sarah was thrilled when Shandy told her the news. 'I knew you could do it!' she enthused. 'Does that mean you can go on living here?'

Shandy nodded. 'Assuming I can make it as a Giles model,' she said. 'I've only signed a probationary contract until I prove myself.'

'Of course you will! You mark my words, before long, you'll have half the men in Adelaide swooning at your feet and inviting you to so many parties, you won't even see your flat for weeks on end. You'll be so much in demand, you won't have time to worry over your broken heart.'

In one way, Sarah proved to be correct. There were no playboys swooning at her feet, of course, but she did come home so exhausted that she fell into a dreamless sleep, too tired even to conjure up her Greek pirate.

Her first assignment was parading summer fashions for an exclusive Glenelg fashion designer. The parades were the disco type, in which the models moved energetically to music, dancing rather than walking up and down the catwalk. Keeping in time to the beat, while showing off the clothes to best advantage as she had been taught at the

Academy, made her feel like a mental octopus, trying to keep her mind on a dozen things at once.

This was followed by a shopping centre promotion, the most punishing and least sought-after assignment of the lot. Changing rooms were nearly always inadequate and schedules hopelessly rushed. Added to which, the audiences seldom gave the models their full attention. Even while the parade was in full swing, children played around the foot of the stage and demonstrators with portable microphones vied with the compère for the attention of the shoppers.

Still, it was during one such parade that Shandy attracted the attention of a photographer from one of the Sunday newspapers. He snapped her as she whirled across the stage in a cloud of spotted organdy, and the photo appeared in the next Sunday's edition.

'Your first appearance in print,' Sarah told her excitedly as she came rushing down with the newspaper in her hands.

'Tomorrow's fish wrappers,' Shandy said, trying to sound blasée, but in truth she was as delighted as Sarah about the picture. She was even more delighted when she rang the booking secretary at the agency next day.

'Your bit of publicity has done you some good, it seems,' the woman told her over the phone.

'In what way?'

'The designer of the dress you were photographed in needs a temporary house model and has asked for you.'

After the shopping centre stint, a spell as a house model sounded blissful. No rushing about on public transport to reach some isolated shopping centre. No cramped changing rooms under staircases. And no children screaming their way through the parade. 'When do I start?' she asked.

'Next Monday, when his regular girl goes on holiday.'

After the shopping centres, the assignment proved to be
a breeze. The girls had to be on hand in case the designer
needed to test-fit a new garment or wanted them to show
off a garment to a client in the salon. Other than that, they
passed the time reading and gossiping in the changing
room. Shandy knew she wouldn't like to spend all her days
like this, but right now it was a pleasant novelty. The only
drawback was the time it gave her to think about the mess
her love life was in.

She had faced the reality that she was far from being
'over' Russell, although she had dutifully tried to date
someone she met in the course of her work. The man had
been pleasant and companionable, but the only time he
kissed her, she had shied away like a startled colt. It was as
if Russell was standing on the sidelines, watching and
laughing at her. 'You'll be kissing him and wishing it was
me,' he seemed to whisper in her ear. The worst of it was,
he was right. Not even Jordan, for all his good looks and
forceful personality, had been able to arouse her as Russell
had. Her body throbbed with sensation at the memory.
Would she never get him out of her system?

'Wake up, dreamy, we're wanted.'

She stirred at Laura's touch. The other girl had worked
for the designer for some time, but had gladly shown the
newcomer the ropes, so they had become good friends.

'What is it this time?' Shandy asked.

'VIP,' Laura informed her. 'You'll be pleased to
know it's the mystery client who ordered the stunning
gown.'

Shandy knew which gown Laura meant. It was a
magnificent wedding gown they had both been drooling
over. No-one knew for whom it had been designed, only

that it was a VIP. One with masses of money, Laura had observed, since the gown was the most expensive design the salon had ever been asked to produce.

'Who gets to wear The Gown?' Shandy asked.

'Sorry, love, my privilege,' Laura said, smiling to take any malice out of her words. 'You can do the going-away outfit.'

This was fair enough, since Laura was the permanent model here, along with the other girl who was away on holidays. Shandy gasped when Laura emerged a short while later in the nearly-completed gown. It was the most beautiful dress Shandy had ever seen, and was created from tier after tier of hand-made lace over a silk under-dress, with a revealing caped neckline and a satin cummerbund which emphasised the wearer's waistline.

'Oh, Laura!' she sighed.

'I know. I'd give anything to trade places with the girl who gets to wear this gown,' Laura agreed.

The going-away outfit that Shandy was to model was stunningly attractive, if not as breathtaking as the wedding gown. It was in richly textured coffee-coloured linen and comprised a divided skirt and matching edge-to-edge jacket worn over a cream raw-silk blouse.

'Ready?' Laura asked over her shoulder. Shandy nodded. 'Well, here goes. At least we get to find out who the special client is at last.'

To create the proper atmosphere, the manageress played a tape of the Wedding March as the girls entered the salon. Laura, looking splendid in the gown, walked ahead of Shandy, suiting her slow paces to the music. At first, she blocked Shandy's view of the client who was seated in the gilt chaise longue at the opposite side of the room. It was a man, which surprised her since she had expected a dewy-eyed bride. Probably the bride's father, she thought dismissively, keeping her eyes demurely downcast, waiting for the proper moment to show off her outfit.

Then her breath caught in her throat as she lifted her gaze and looked straight into Russell's dark eyes. Why did he, of all people, have to be the mystery client? Her step faltered and a sob was wrenched from her. She had to force herself to complete her circuit of the salon.

'Hello, Shandy,' Russell said in an undertone as she passed near to him.

The caressing way he said her name destroyed all her remaining poise. With a strangled cry, she turned and fled back towards the changing room, heedless of the startled gaze of the salon manageress. In the sanctuary of the dressing room, she slammed the door shut and bolted it, then stripped off the wedding clothes which his presence had cruelly mocked. Quickly, she dressed again in her own clothes.

For whom was he ordering the most costly wedding gown in Australia? Was it for Helen Crossley, his housekeeper who had ordered Shandy away from Russell? Or was it for one of the other women he was reputed to be seeing at Ceduna? She tried to tell herself she didn't care, he could marry whom he wished, but the tears coursing down her cheeks unmasked the brave lie for what it was.

There was a hammering on the locked door. 'Shandy, open this door. I've got to talk to you.'

'Go away!' she said through her tears. If she let him in, she just might break down and tell him how much she loved him, only to have him taunt her with the name of his prospective bride. She couldn't bear it, she couldn't! Like a cornered animal, she looked wildly around the room. The fire escape!

Without giving herself a chance to reconsider, she opened the window and stepped out onto the rickety metal staircase that led down to an alley at the rear of the building. So intent was she on negotiating the narrow steps down to the ground; that she failed to notice a car glide almost silently along the alley and come to a stop underneath her.

No sooner had she jumped the remaining few feet to the ground, than she was grabbed from behind and thrust unceremoniously into the back of the car. The door slammed shut behind her and in despair, she saw the locks go down automatically, operated by the driver. She was trapped.

'Now will you listen to me?' Russell said mildly.

She whirled towards him, choked with fury. 'What gives you the right to snatch me off the street like this?'

'I told you, I had to talk to you.'

She averted her face. 'I think you made yourself perfectly clear when we last met. I recall you ordered me out of your life on that occasion.'

'Well, now I'm ordering you back in,' he said with maddening good cheer.

'You're very good at giving orders, aren't you?' she retorted scathingly. 'But this time I'm not going to obey you so readily. You can't keep me a prisoner forever, and this time I intend to go to the police and have you charged with kidnapping.'

He was unperturbed. 'That will be difficult, since a wife can't testify against her husband.'

What was he talking about? 'Wife? You *must* be mad!' she seethed.

'We shall soon see.'

While she had been arguing with him, she hadn't noticed the car travelling smoothly towards the Adelaide airport. She had an uncanny sense of déjà vu as the driver, whom she recognised as Les, the pilot who had been a party to kidnapping her the first time, steered the car into a parking space at the airport. 'Where are you taking me?' she demanded of Russell.

'You'll soon find out. Just relax and enjoy the journey.'

Relax and enjoy . . . now she knew he was mad! For the second time, she was being forcibly abducted by him and flown off to God knew where without any explanation or by-your-leave. His reference to a wife had made her doubly nervous. What sort of game was he playing? Surely he didn't intend to force her into marriage to assuage his colossal ego? In all the time she had struggled against acknowledging her love for him, this was what she had most feared—that he would use his wealth and power to bend her to his will, riding rough-shod over her feelings. Well, it wasn't going to work. She intended to fight him every step of the way.

As before, they proceeded from the carpark to the private plane with no hindrance from any authorities, putting paid to any hope she might have had of enlisting outside help.

Once again, they were airborne and she was entirely at his mercy. This time, however, she wasn't frightened, so much as trembling with fury over his arrogant treatment of her.

When he offered her a drink from a portable bar at the back of the plane, she declined icily. He shrugged. 'Suit yourself. But it's a long trip to Chedoona Downs.'

Chedoona? He was taking her back to his property on the Eyre Peninsula. 'Why are you doing this?' she asked miserably.

'Because you and I have a lot of talking to do, and you wouldn't let me say everything I have to say in Adelaide.'

What could he possibly have to say to her? she wondered despondently. Hadn't he said it all in that final, cruel directive which had haunted her ever since? She closed her eyes and pretended to doze until she felt a change in the plane's progress; then she looked out of the window.

Underneath her, the pink-tinged clouds parted to reveal the serrated coastline of the Eyre Peninsula. As the plane lost height, the triangle of land jutting out into the Bight came rushing up to meet them, then they banked and headed inland, passing over the arid Nullarbor Plains—the 'Heartbreak Plains' which had, so far, more than lived up to their nickname for her.

Dully, she absorbed the impact of landing and sat still while Russell undid her seatbelt. Maybe if she turned herself into an unfeeling robot, she would somehow survive this ordeal. At least she could make herself so difficult to be with that Russell would be glad to release her and return her to Adelaide.

Her lack of response didn't seem to worry him at all, as he loaded his luggage into a waiting Range Rover. She had only the handbag she'd taken with her when she fled from the salon, so it wasn't long before they were once again cresting the hill that led down to the homestead.

She had to restrain an aching sensation as she was confronted with the familiar cluster of buildings. She was an interloper here, brought for whatever purpose Russell had in mind—so she mustn't start to have any feeling of warmth towards the place.

'Welcome back, Shandy,' Helen Crossley said warmly as she walked hesitantly into the family room of the blue-tinged stone homestead. Robin hurried across the room and bent to plant a kiss on her cheek.

'We're all very happy for you, love.'

Bewildered, she looked back at Russell, but he offered no explanation for the odd greetings. The biggest surprise was still to come. As she stood looking around her in confusion, Barbara hurtled across the room and wrapped her arms around Shandy. 'Congratulations, Shandy,' she said through tears of laughter. 'I'm so happy for you. Imagine! I'm going to be your step-daughter . . . me!'

'Step-daughter? But I don't . . .'

Only then did Russell take pity on her and step forward. 'Just a minute, everyone,' he said good-naturedly. 'Don't you think it would be better if I proposed first?'

For a moment, they looked at Russell in stricken silence. 'Oops, seems we put our collective foot in it,' Robin said, speaking for all of them.'

'We thought you'd have settled everything on the way here,' Barbara said sheepishly.

'Settled what? Will someone please tell me what's going on?' Shandy said desperately.

For answer, Russell took her arm and led her outside, where he pushed her gently into a cane armchair beside the pool. 'What they're all trying to make you understand is that I love you and want to marry you,' he said quietly.

She stared at him in astonishment. 'Love me? How can you love me when you don't even trust me?'

He frowned. 'I was coming to that. I owe you an apology for thinking you could ever be in cahoots with a bitch like Della. I should have known you weren't the type.'

'How did you find out the truth?'

'Barbara told me. After Della broke down and told her the true circumstances of her birth. I believe you heard the whole story from Anna.'

She nodded, and a cold hand clutched at her heart. 'Della *told* her?' she whispered in horror. 'Poor Barbara. It must have come as a terrible shock after all this time.'

'It did,' he agreed grimly. 'She was in a dreadful state

when she came to see me. Luckily I've been able to convince her that it doesn't make any difference to how I feel about her. As far as I'm concerned, she's my daughter, no matter what happened before she was born.'

'But why would Della tell her now?'

'My guess is she was hoping to drive a permanent wedge between Barbara and me. Instead, it helped Barbara to realise how she's been misled all these years. She's determined to make up for all the years we've lost because of Della—and I intend to give her a father she can be proud of.'

'How could she be otherwise?' Shandy asked, surprising herself. Then she wrinkled her brow. 'But I still don't understand what this has got to do with you and me.'

'Everything,' he explained. 'Once I knew I'd been wrong about you and Della, I started to wonder what else I'd been wrong about. I went to see your friend, Jordan Cole.'

She clutched a hand to her mouth. 'Oh!'

'Yes, oh! He didn't strike me as offering much competition for your love. In fact, he gave me his blessing to carry you off at the first opportunity. Does that sound like a jealous lover to you?' Dumbly, she shook her head. 'It didn't to me either, so I came to the conclusion that you made up the business about sleeping with him to hide the truth from me.'

'There isn't any truth,' she said desperately. How could Jordan have betrayed her like this?

'Oh no? Then what about that painting of me that Cole had on show in his studio?'

Painting? She felt hot colour suffusing her face as she remembered she had left the portrait of the Greek pirate at Orana. She had remembered that the pictures were still in Jordan's studio when she was half-way back to Adelaide, but had decided to leave them there until she could go back to collect them. 'You saw the painting?' she whispered.

'I saw much more. In that picture, I saw a lot of love that was being denied to me. That love belongs to me, Shandy, and I want it. I want you. Why do you think I had that gown made?'

He was saying the very things she had dreamed of hearing ever since she walked away from him in Adelaide, ordered out of his life forever. Still, she was confused. 'I . . . I can't give you my love, Russell. Because you don't want it as a gift—you want to take it as a right.'

'I know my background scares you,' he said levelly. 'After what happened to your parents, it's hardly surprising. But I'm not going to let you use it as an excuse any longer. If you'll agree to marry me, I'm quite prepared to sign over everything I own to Barbara right now. We'll move to a cottage in Thevenard or wherever you say.'

She could hardly believe what she was hearing. He was willing to give up everything for her. Her last reason for refusing him had been removed. But there was still an unanswered question. 'What about Helen Crossley?' she asked.

'What about her?' he asked, plainly baffled.

'I think she believes you intend to marry her,' she said. 'She . . . she warned me off you the last time I was here.'

To her surprise, he laughed uproariously. 'As if any man could ever take the place of her beloved Arthur,' he said dismissively. 'Have you considered that she might have been afraid you had designs on her *son*—who, as you now know, is spoken for—and she didn't want you to get hurt?'

'She was talking about *Robin*?' He nodded and she

blushed furiously. 'What a fool I've been—over everything.'

'I hope that means over me, too, because I meant it when I said I want you as my wife, Shandy Farrer. These last few days have been hell without you.' He raked a hand through his hair, tousling it. 'I know I've got no right to ask you—I'm too old for you, but I swear I'll do anything in my power to make you happy.'

'Nothing could make me happier than I am right now,' she confessed.

His smile widened. 'You mean that? Oh, my darling, does that mean you could learn to love me in time?'

'I learned to do that almost as soon as I came here,' she admitted. 'But I thought there was too much against us.'

'Not any more,' he said firmly. 'Shall I give everything away so we can be married and move to Thevenard?'

'You don't have to do that,' she said. 'I've had lots of time to think since I left you, and I finally decided you were right. It wasn't your age or your money—none of that matters, I can see that now. I was running away from the enormity of entrusting my love to another person. After what happened to the only two other people I loved . . . I was afraid. As for the money, the lesson was there for me to see all along, in my parents' marriage. But the way they died blinded me to the truth. They were blissfully happy when they had nothing, and when they had everything—because they loved each other. It finally made me understand that it isn't what you have in the bank that counts, so much as what you have in your heart.'

'In that case, Charlotte Farrer, you're already a very rich woman,' he told her.

'And it's all yours for the taking,' she responded shyly. 'For richer, for poorer . . .'

Unable to restrain himself a moment longer, he drew

her into his arms and crushed his lips to hers. The warmth of his body communicated itself to her, igniting fires of passion deep in her soul, which she knew would take a lifetime to quench. 'Until death us do part,' he finished for her.

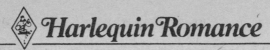

Harlequin Romance

Coming Next Month

2791 HUNTER'S SNARE Emily Ruth Edwards
Faking an engagement to protect her boss from an old flame
seems an outrageous idea for a secretary—until she needs
protection of her own from Connecticut's most dynamic
new businessman.

2792 IMPRESSIONS Tracy Hughes
A Manhattan image consultant has trouble finding the right
look for the host of the TV network's new public affairs show.
Her client thinks he's just fine the way he is—for the network
and for her!

2793 SEPARATE LIVES Carolyn Jantz
Their financial problems were solved by marriage, and love
was an added bonus. Now doubts and the very contract that
brought them together threaten to drive them apart.

2794 CALL OF THE MOUNTAIN Miriam MacGregor
The faster an editor completes her assignment, the faster she
can leave behind a New Zealand station and her boss's
ridiculous accusations. If only his opinion of her wasn't
so important....

2795 IMPULSIVE CHALLENGE Margaret Mayo
When a secretary, who has no illusions about her "love 'em and
leave 'em" boss, finds herself jealous of his glamorous
neighbor, she's shocked. She's fallen in love—the thing she
vowed never to do again.

2796 SAFARI HEARTBREAK Gwen Westwood
This mother doesn't object to her son's yearly visits to his
father, until her mother-in-law's illness forces her into making
the trek back to Africa—scene of her greatest heartbreak...her
greatest happiness.

Available in October wherever paperback books are sold, or
through Harlequin Reader Service.

In the U.S.
P.O. Box 1397
Buffalo, N.Y.
14240-1397

In Canada
P.O. Box 2800, Postal Station A
5170 Yonge Street
Willowdale, Ontario M2N 6J3

Could she find love as a mail-order bride?

MARIANNE WILLMAN

PIECES OF SKY

In the Arizona of 1873, Nora O'Shea is caught between life with a contemptuous, arrogant husband and her desperate love for Roger LeBeau, half-breed Comanche Indian scout and secret freedom fighter.